THE BODY

IN THE

PADDY FIELD

NADISHKA ALOYSIUS

CHAPTER ONE

I **WAS** lost.

Google Maps had brought me to the edge of a paddy field.

I glared at my phone and flung the unhelpful device into the passenger seat beside me. Resisting the urge to scream I vented my frustration on the steering wheel instead pummelling it with both fists. An ear shattering PAARP tore through the silence scaring some white birds into flight. I was tempted to lean on the horn once more (on purpose rather than by accident this time); instead, I clutched the wheel and forced myself to breathe deeply. The silence was deafening.

Stop thinking in clichés and find the damn house! What's the bet that bloody woman gave me the wrong address. She hasn't changed much from when we were in university!

I took another breath, forced myself to calm down, sank back into the leather upholstery, and flexed my fingers. Being cooped up in a small vehicle for almost three hours had turned my knees to lead. *Escaping one stifling situation only to land in another. Well done, Kiyama!*

Deciding to walk the kinks out of my muscles, I parked on the side of the offending pathway and got down. The air smelt fresh and damp. The dirt road was dark and wet because of the thunder showers the night before. Wading gingerly through the squelching mud to the edge of the paddy field I gazed into the distance. Low mountains on the horizon were topped by an incongruously perfect blue sky. There was no sign of rain today, yet. *But it is the monsoon season. With my luck, the roughly cut drains will flood and I'll be swept away in the deluge!*

My 360-degree inspection of the place ended at my car. My jaw dropped – it was dotted in brown and looked like an overweight leopard on wheels! *It's unlikely they have a car wash in town, and I'll have to clean this myself!*

Despite my black mood the beauty of my surroundings

worked its magic: draining my irritability away and leaving me more relaxed. I was ready to resume my journey and find my way back into civilization. Feeling a stab of guilt, I rooted around under the passenger seat for my phone. *I'll have to be careful with this. They probably don't have a good phone repair shop either.*

Closing Google Maps, I counted to five and reopened the app. After double checking the printout lying on my dashboard I typed 'Monara Para, Parkaduwa' making doubly sure the spelling was accurate. The arrow swivelled like a demented weathervane and finally pointed back the way I had just driven into this dead end. *Typical of my life right now.*

The digital numbers of the clock on my phone informed me that it was 4:30 p.m. and I had better find Vino's house soon, or at least a hotel to stay the night.

Reversing inch by inch out of that cul-de-sac left me with a crick in my neck and the beginnings of a migraine, and I swore to buy a push bicycle as soon as I was settled in. I turned the annoying female voice on and obediently turned left and right until I lost all sense of direction, hoping she knew where she was taking me. Surprisingly, within ten minutes I was back in the centre of the small town. The bars on the phone showed a good signal, so I decided to give Vino a call.

The phone seemed to ring forever before a chirpy voice

answered.

"Hi, Vino? It's Kiyama," was all I managed to get out before she was off.

"Kiy? Where in heaven's name are you? I prepared lunch! And you know how I feel about cooking! Do you know what time it is? It may be lunchtime somewhere in Europe but it's definitely not lunchtime in this country."

I jumped in when she paused for air. "Vino, I got lost. I still am, I think. Anyway, I'm back in the centre of the town, near the main bus halt. Is your road even on Google Maps?"

Vino laughed. "I've never tried Google Maps here so maybe it isn't. You just park the car where you are, and I'll be there in a jiffy. You're still driving that yellow Maruti, right?"

"Yes."

"Great, then I won't miss you. See you soon!"

"Is there…" I started but she had already hung up. I sighed for what felt like the hundredth time today. I had wanted to ask her if there was anywhere I could grab a snack while I waited. But on second thought, that query may have got her back onto the topic of the missed lunch date.

Getting out of the car I glanced around. Parkaduwa was typical of many small towns in Sri Lanka with one main road driving through and lots of little lanes that took you to the middle of nowhere. Small shops lined the main road, most of which were closed for the holiday. I read the signs as I leaned against my vehicle. Saradha Stores (looked like a small grocery shop). Harini Textiles (obviously a clothes shop). Richy Bakers (looked like a small pastry shop with local buns and shorteats). My stomach grumbled. I had finished the last snack bar during the drive hours ago. Maybe the impending headache was a sign of low blood sugar. I considered my choices. I really needed something in my system, but was I brave enough to eat from a small kade? Who knew how hygienic such places were? Also, I'm not a fan of very oily food, and I doubted if they had anything to suit my palate. Coming to a decision I crossed the road and entered the grocery store. Luckily, they had some packets of Milo lined up on the counter and I bought two in relief.

Back in my car I rolled the shutters down and watched a handful of local residents eye me suspiciously as they passed by. It was extremely quiet, even for a Sunday. There were so many buses parked at the depot, I wondered if any were running today. It looked like they took the holiday very seriously here, unlike in Colombo where everything functioned through the weekend.

I checked my phone again. The numbers 5:15 p.m. glared at

me. *What could possibly be keeping my friend?*

Some people wonder why I do not wear a wristwatch. I just cannot be bothered taking it off at night and slapping it on my wrist again the next day. My phone is always with me. It lights up in the dark. The numbers are easy to read. Life is much more efficient that way.

I idly flicked through my messages. There was nothing from Andy. It was ten days now since I last spoke to him, and I wondered if my abrupt departure had shocked him into silence. The sun was low in the sky when I noticed that the phone battery was almost dead. *Great! No food, no phone, and nowhere to go!*

Adjusting the car seat so that I could stretch out and lie back I closed my eyes for a few seconds and pictured my friend, Vinodhini Dias, with whom I planned to spend the next few weeks. She had worn her shoulder length hair in a pony tail the last time I saw her, and I wondered if she still sported the same style. Unlikely, since I had gone from waist length tresses to a shoulder length bob in the same period of time.

Vino had been the tallest of our gang at university. They had even invited her to join the women's basketball team purely because of her height. I grinned to myself as an image of Laurel and Hardy popped into my head. That is what the two of us look like – her Laurel to my Hardy. I sighed. At five feet four inches in height, I was not short (by Sri Lankan standards) but I knew I had a lot to live up to next to my friend. I groaned. *Cracking bad jokes to oneself is a sure sign of mind-numbing boredom!*

I had lost myself in a book (I always carry one in my bag) when a tap on the windshield interrupted my solitude. I looked up in alarm to see Vino grinning like the Cheshire Cat. She was leaning her tall lanky frame against the car, and her long hair was tied back in a plait.

"Nose in a book as always, I see," she commented, as I climbed out and gave her a hug.

"Vinodhini Dias! What took you so long? I've been dying here!"

"Hey, you'd better get used to long periods of nothing if you're going to live here!" came her immediate rejoinder.

It was then that I noticed that she was steering a bicycle. And that she looked great: healthy and carefree, a far cry from the harassed and hassled accountant I had known in Colombo.

"You cycled here?" I asked. "No wonder I had to suffer a long period of nothing!"

"Healthy living and the village life. Give it a try and you won't regret it!"

I climbed back into my car.

"Okay, then. You cycle and I'll follow. I hope the lunch you cooked is still edible, by the way, I'm starving!"

Half an hour and an uncountable number of twisty lanes full of potholes later, I was tucking into Vino's rice and curry. The house was so far off the beaten track, it had no number and therefore did not show on Google Maps. When I asked Vino how she got her mail, she shrugged and said, "I rarely get any mail. And the house goes by the name 'Komarika Lodge'."

"Do you have an aloe vera plantation in your back yard?" I spluttered as I gulped some water.

"I inherited the property, you know. I had no say in the name!"

"Sorry, just kidding. It's a lovely place," I said as I finished off the last of my chicken.

That was the truth. I had seen kohomba, jak, mango, and guava as I manoeuvred through the driveway which curved in from one gate, under a portico of the bungalow and wound its way out another. The garden looked well-tended and clean, and I wondered whether Vino worked on it herself or paid a labourer from the village to complete the chores.

The house looked too modern to be an ancestral walauwa. Instead of showcasing low ceilings, intricate lattice work, and dark musty interiors the house was airy and open with French windows on one side overlooking the garden. The living room cum dining room was one large hall and had the usual eclectic collection of furniture that made most Sri Lankan homes look like bric-a-brac stores. The walls were full of nondescript paintings selected more for their ability to fill a vacant space than artistic merit. Two or three rooms lead out from the central hall. That reminded me that my belongings were still in the car, and I needed to unpack.

With Vino's help I lugged my bags into the house, and I was soon ensconced in my own bedroom. She perched on the bed while I explored the cupboard and dresser and started settling in. I saw her taking in my two large suitcases and I knew she was itching to question me. So, I took a break from fussing needlessly with my clothes and seated myself in an armchair in the corner, ready to face the inquisition.

"I can see you're dying to ask. So, ask."

She looked momentarily uncomfortable, but then regained her natural curiosity. "Is the rest of your stuff at the house with

Andy?"

I fidgeted. I had not really had a heart to heart with any of my friends in the last few months. Or to be honest, in the last few years. "Vino, I want to thank you for letting me crash at your place like this. I know it was all very last minute…"

She brushed my comment aside with, "Of course it's no trouble! I'm all alone in this massive house and I haven't really made many friends in the area. So, you're doing me a favour by staying here. And you don't need to explain anything to me right now if you don't want to."

"But I want to… I need to… to talk to someone." I paused, collecting my thoughts. "It was all a shock to me. I mean Andy and I have been married for almost ten years now. And to find out that he was having an affair…"

I felt my eyes burn. "My eyes are always tearing at the wrong times!" I said, making a feeble attempt at a joke.

Vino smiled, and asked gently, "How did you find out?"

"There was no lipstick on his collar, or anything dramatic. I just happened to walk into a restaurant that they were in. I was with Sulochana, do you remember her?" My throat clenched at the recollection. "It was actually a series of unfortunate events. I wanted to go for something western, but she wanted Japanese, so we tossed a coin and ended up at her choice of restaurant. And the rest, as they say, is history."

"But he could have been just having a meal with a friend, right?"

I snorted. "Not the way she was dressed. And not the way they were holding hands and staring into each other's eyes."

She giggled, and then clapped a hand over her mouth. "Sorry. So, what did you do when you saw them?"

"What I *wanted* to do was to throw my drink at him! What I *did* do was finish my meal with as much dignity as I could muster. Sulo saw them too and wanted to leave but I decided to just get it over with. I went home and took down the two largest suitcases we had and stuffed them with everything I could think of. I didn't want to stay with my mother, and I couldn't think of any friends whose doorstep I could just turn up at, so I checked into a hotel."

"Were you at the hotel when you called?" Vino asked, her eyes wide.

"Yes. I was checking out some idyllic village escapes online, and you just popped into my mind. I'm sorry if I kind of invited myself here, but…"

"Of course not, Kiy! I sensed something was up when you asked if you could come over for a few days. I'm just glad you confided in me… And I hope you get things sorted out."

I'm not the most physical of people, but I accepted her hug with good grace.

"Oh, by the way, does Andy know where you are?" she asked as she drew back.

I stifled a laugh. "I left him a note."

"A note?!"

"I told him I saw him at the restaurant, and I need a break to get my head straight. And I told him to figure out what he wants, that I'll be in touch."

"You'll be in touch? That's a good one! Did you give him my address?"

"God, no! I don't want the bastard turning up here! Of course, I now know there's no chance in hell of that happening because the place is not even on the map!" I clicked my fingers. "Hey, that's a thought. Maybe I should send him an address and send him on a wild goose chase!"

Vino laughed. "If he even bothers to come after you."

That thought sobered me. I hadn't really thought of what I would do if Andy decided he did not want to get back together. Divorce is such an ugly word, and I did not think I was brave enough to venture down that road.

Vino must have sensed my discomfort because she changed

the topic. "So, now that you are here do you have any thoughts on what exactly you're going to do? You weren't working in Colombo, no?"

"Luckily, no, or I wouldn't have been able to take off like this. I gave up my job at that international school last year. I guess once I get back to civilization, I can find another job. I mean, English literature is a subject I can teach in any school, right? Until then, I'm living off my savings – reckless and carefree!"

"Huh! Back to civilization! I like that!" Vino objected in mock exasperation. "But seriously, though, maybe you could start giving afterschool classes. You'd have more flexibility that way."

"Yes, I thought of that. But enough about me! Tell me what you've been up to."

She got up and moved out of the room. "Come on. I think we both need a cup of coffee. Let's sit in the veranda."

CHAPTER TWO

A FEW minutes later, clasping a hot mug in my hand, I listened as Vino shared her life.

"I'm still running the rubber plantation. It's easier now that I know the ropes a little. My uncle obviously had no doubts about my abilities, or those of the management, when he left the plantation to me."

"I remember your shock when you realised you had to live out here!" I said. "But the move has done you good. I guess turning your back on Colombo has its benefits. Is the plantation close by?"

"It's down the road. I cycle to keep fit, and also because the roads, you know…"

"Are so full of holes," I completed with a wince. My back and legs were still sore from all that bouncing around. I shuddered to think what they had done to my car.

"And what about your love life?" I asked with a grin.

Vino laughed out loud. "Love life? Here? I guess I could take up with some guy at the rubber factory, or the research centre, or a teacher at the school, but there's no one I fancy. And I'm not getting into a relationship with anyone from the village. Farming is not my thing!"

"Oh, come on, I can picture you mucking about in a muddy paddy field…"

She shuddered. "No, thank you!"

As we relaxed into a companionable silence, sipping our coffee and listening to the birdsong in the garden, a sense a contentment crept over me. However much she protested, I knew I was imposing on my friend's life and I was lucky she had agreed to have me over. I could not imagine where I would be if she had not.

That night, I slept like a baby.

I was stress free for the first time in weeks, and I knew I had made the correct decision. Some would argue that you cannot run away from your troubles. I believed recharging my batteries and taking a holiday would clear my mind. Who knows – I may have an epiphany while walking through the woods. I smiled to myself as I murmured the words of Robert Frost.

> "The woods are lovely, dark and deep,
>
> But I have promises to keep,
>
> And miles to go before I sleep,
>
> And miles to go before I sleep…"

Once a teacher, always a teacher.

My bedroom was simple, but cozy. The double bed was covered in an unadorned white sheet. There were no extravagant paintings or sculptures like you would find in a hotel room. The only other furniture was a writing table, a cupboard, and a dresser – all made of solid dark wood. The room sported two windows: one looking out to the garden and the other to the back yard. Flimsy lace curtains fluttered in the wind created by the old-fashioned ceiling fan that, despite its age, cooled the room comfortably.

Lying on my own in the large bed, I was able to truly ease the tension in my body and mind. I have never been one to play soothing music and light scented candles, but the calm and quiet night devoid of the incessant hustle and bustle of city life did wonders to my psyche. The chirp and buzz of insects flurrying around outside were all the music I needed to lull me to sleep.

I awoke to the sound of human activity outside. Yawning I glanced at the bedside clock - it was 8.30 a.m! As I struggled to focus and kickstart my sleepy brain it dawned on me that today was Monday – and Vino may have already left for work. After our little chat last evening I had forgotten to ask her about her housekeeping arrangements and wondered if I would have to scrounge up my meals for the day. A quick turn in the adjoining bathroom, and I was ready. Jumping into a pair of linen shorts and a sleeveless blouse I made my way into the main living area of the house. Noises of cooking were coming from the kitchen, so I hesitantly poked my head in through the door. A large woman dressed in a voluminous flower-print cheettha redi dress was busy at the stove. She had iron grey hair pulled back in a bun, buckteeth, and hard black eyes.

"Good morning?" I ventured.

She spun around waving a frying pan. "Ah! Good morning Madam! Vino Miss told me a friend came over yesterday night, but the house was so quiet I thought she was joking! Well, here you are. I have put bread and pol sambol on the dining table. I can make an egg or anything else you want…"

Keeping my distance from the cooking utensil, which was being brandished like a weapon, I smiled. "My name is Kiyama. And, please, call me Miss like you do for Vino, rather than Madam. I'm not that old!"

"Yes," she said, eyeing me up and down. "I can see that."

Simmering a little at her presumptuousness, I turned and sat at the large dining table where the promised breakfast was already laid out. There was fresh baker's bread (a wonderful change from the packaged sandwich bread widely available back home), a reddish-orange pol sambol that promised a fiery kick to the taste buds, and some fruit.

I looked towards the kitchen doorway and waved at the cook, "This is great. Thank you."

I had barely swallowed one mouthful before she appeared at my side.

"So, *Miss*, are you staying long?"

I tore my bread into small pieces.

"Maybe. Nothing has been decided yet."

"Are you an old friend of our Miss?"

"Yes."

"Are your husband and children joining us also?"

That was the last straw. *What did it matter to her whether I was married or not? Whether or not I had children?*

I looked down at my left hand. I still wore my ring. I should have taken the damn thing off before I left Colombo! But then, the mark of the band would have made the cook even more curious. Swallowing a mouthful of sambol I plastered what I hoped was a friendly smile on my face and said, "This is very hot. Can I have some water?"

She gave me a searching look and bustled away into the kitchen. She soon returned with a jug and glass. Setting them down on the table she announced, "I'm making rice and curry for lunch. Vino Miss usually comes home in the afternoon for a few hours. I'll remember and lessen the chillie for you."

With that she turned and swept into the kitchen.

I wanted to bury my head in my hands. I did not know whether to laugh or cry, so I opted instead to finish my meal seated outside. Hopefully, relaxing on the veranda would dampen the volcano waiting to erupt.

The day was bright and sunny, and I pushed the insolent cook to the back of my mind as I surveyed the garden. It was larger than I had first supposed. In the centre was a well-maintained lawn. Fruit trees ranged along the sides closer to the boundary wall. A bird bath decorated a corner. Dusting my fingers, I rose and followed the sandy driveway that curved from the entrance gate to the exit. When I peered out, no one was visible on the lane outside. So, I made my way to the left, following the sounds of digging.

An old man in a sarong and vest was industriously plying the earth by some wooden fences. *Vegetables! Vino had her own plot of vegetables!* That brightened my mood. Hoping that he was not in any way related to the cook, I walked up to the gardener and cleared my throat.

"Err…Hello."

He did not look up and he did not stop digging.

"I'm looking forward to eating your homegrown vegetables."

Silence.

"They are so much healthier than what you get at the supermarket, no?"

Nothing.

"Which vegetables are in season now?" I persisted, hoping that an open-ended question would prompt an answer.

He angled his chin towards some plants on the right.

I could see some small lumps of purple hanging off the thin branches.

"Are those brinjals?" I asked, though I could not think of any other vegetables of that vivid colour.

He grunted.

I felt like cheering! *Finally, a response!* I tried again.

"Do you work here every day? The garden looks really good."

No response.

I gave up.

One worker inside the house with verbal diarrhoea and an insatiable curiosity, another outside who acted like a speechless automaton! I turned to continue my stroll hoping that these were not the sum of humanity living in the town of Parkaduwa.

I was seated again on the veranda with a book in hand when Vino cycled in and leaned her bike against a wall. She had a trendy sling bag across her body, and she was dressed in trousers, a blouse, and sandals.

"Your sunglasses don't go with that ensemble," I called out as she approached.

"And you look urban chic," she replied.

"Your cook didn't approve," I commented, as she dropped into the lounge chair next to me.

"That's Manike. She comes in daily to cook and clean. I knew I should have introduced you before I left, but I didn't have the heart to wake you up. I just warned her that I had a guest and hoped for the best."

I burst out laughing. "Manike? Really? Manike in Ratnapura is a bit much, no? And, if she's a diamond in the rough, then I'm a monkey's uncle!"

"Why? What did she say?"

"It's more the look she gave me that put me on edge. Is she always this nosy?"

Vino covered her mouth with her hand, her eyes twinkling. "Why, did she ask you where your husband is?"

"Yes! And if I have any children!"

Vino was enjoying this. "Oh dear! She pulled out all the stops, didn't she? I shouldn't have told her to make you feel welcome!"

Seeing my expression, she went on, "You should see your face! Darling, if you want to spend time in a small town or village you must get used to the nosy parkers and gossip mongers. They're part of the natural landscape."

"More fauna than flora, I think." I looked at the garden. "I also met your gardener. An old chap? He's the polar opposite, isn't he? Didn't say a word."

"Yes, that's Somasiri. He doesn't talk much to anyone. But he's got amazing green fingers. All our fruits, flowers, and veggies are thanks to his magic."

We both turned as Manike came out of the house.

"Miss Vino, you're early today. Lunch is ready. I cut down on the chillie since your friend can't manage the spices."

"Thank you, Manike," Vino replied solemnly, making sure not to catch my eye. "We'll be right in."

She arched an eyebrow at me once the cook left.

"My fault. I wanted to get rid of her, so I asked for some water," I sighed.

Vino patted my arm. "There, there. You'll get used to their idiosyncrasies. So…what do you want to do this evening?"

"Don't you have to return to the plantation?"

"They're more than able to manage without me. I'm still learning the ropes, anyway. None of the courses I took in Colombo prepared me for that job!"

As we ate, Vino took me through the workings of a rubber plantation. I confess, it was not the most entertaining of subject matter, but I felt obliged to understand her world, since she made such an effort to help me figure out mine.

"So, that's how the rubber sap is turned into the everyday objects we use," she concluded as we nibbled some fruit at the end of the meal.

"Wow," I said, "I've got to hand it to you. You have done your homework. To be able to explain all that without reading off a manual is amazing! You know what? I think your uncle knew exactly what he was doing when he left the plantation to you. He knew that you are tenacious and dedicated and even though you knew nothing about the subject, you'd dive right in and give it a shot."

Vino beamed. "Thanks, Kiy. It's nice to be appreciated."

She stopped to wipe her hands on her napkin. "So, what do you want to do on your first full day here? Shall I give you a tour of the town? The shops are all open today."

I almost bounced off my chair. "You kidding? I've been raring to go exploring from morning! Just don't take me down any dead-end lanes that lead to a paddy field!"

CHAPTER THREE

A **FULL STOMACH** and a good night's sleep work wonders on one's perspective of life. The dull Main Street looked colourful and lively that Monday afternoon. Since two of us could not share one push bicycle, we did a leisurely stroll into town. We decided early on that forcing my poor Maruti to bounce around was not an option and purchasing my own set of wheels was our number one priority. As we entered the bicycle shop, I hoped they accepted credit cards, since I was not carrying much in the way of cash. I was already hot and sweaty after the walk and not in the mood to stand in line at the local bank.

My luck was in, and soon we were happily pedalling our way along winding country roads. Vino gave me a few safety tips on cycling as we rode.

1) Always carry your lock and chain as there are no bicycle stands
2) Wear sensible clothes and footwear
3) Invest in a backpack
4) Carry a raincoat if it looks like rain
5) Beware buses since they don't follow any road rules
6) Also watch out for dogs and cows that may wander across your path
7) Avoid impromptu cricket matches whenever you can

Vino was also a good tour guide, regaling me with humorous anecdotes as we cycled.

"That's the local bakery. Apparently, they chose the name Richy in the hopes that they'd make a fortune. They make a good butter cake, but the rest of the food is too oily for my taste. That's the post office. The best gossip can be heard there, or so says our Manike. There's a Buddhist temple up that hill. A couple of decades ago, the entire town was flooded, and everyone sought refuge in the temple premises. And, apparently, one young woman didn't come back down – she stayed on as the head priest's mistress!"

I almost fell off my bike at that piece of news.

"Seriously?" I gasped, as I regained my balance.

"Seriously," replied Vino, "That is the main school in the area," she continued, pointing to a large white building with the words PARKADUWA CENTRAL COLLEGE in large blue letters.

I surveyed the vast open landscape in awe. So much empty space with no high-rise buildings fuelling your claustrophobia… It was heaven. In the distance, I could spot a large old-fashioned three-story building that seemed out of place with its large pillars and ornate gate. "Is that a hotel?" I asked, pointing.

Vino squinted. "Not yet. That used to belong to a gem merchant, but he passed away recently. There is a rumour that his son, who came down from overseas, is turning the place into a hotel. If they have a spa, maybe we could go and indulge ourselves once in a way!"

"That's a great idea but setting that up is going to take ages and it's unlikely I'll be still here."

Vino winked. "You never know! These small-towns tend to grow on you!"

"And…This road leads to Eheliya town, so, that's the end of our tour," she announced, as we reached the top of a rise and surveyed the endless fields. It reminded me of a patchwork quilt in shades of green, dotted in white where birds rested (*storks? I'd have to ask*), each square bordered in muddy brown.

But one square of the quilt had a lot more people hanging around than the others. I could see a mass of bodies, and even a few people running in that direction. Some were pointing into the paddy field. Vehicles were also stopping on the side of the road as curious passers-by decided to examine what was going on. They looked like ants huddled around a morsel of food. I turned to Vino, "Trouble?"

She shaded her eyes against the glare of the sun, replied, "When in Rome..." and started cycling down towards the crowd.

The level of activity had increased by the time we reached our destination, and a dark blue police jeep had pulled up. Two khaki clad policemen jumped down and started making their way through the crowd as we dismounted and locked our bikes. I did not relish the thought of pushing our way through the sweaty bodies, so we hung around the edges hoping to eavesdrop on a productive conversation. It is amazing how much information one can gather by standing still amid a babbling crowd.

"The farmer has only found a dead animal in his field."

"What rubbish! This crowd won't gather for a dead animal!"

"The cops came all the way from Eheliya so something's up."

I nudged Vino and whispered, "Isn't there a police station in town?"

"No," she whispered back, "they're based in the nearest large town ten kilometres down the main A5."

We listened in again, trying to figure out what was happening.

"Maybe it's that girl, you know, the one who ran away from home… Her parents were adamant she didn't leave of her own accord."

"Tcha! That one ran off with her boyfriend! Her parents are too stupid to know what she was up to! If she ever turns up, she will have a baby in her arms!"

The idle speculation cut off as a boy of about twelve years squeezed his way through the milling crowd. One of the men caught him by the arm and asked, "So? What's happening?"

The boy's eyes shone, and he could barely stand still. He flapped his hands in excitement as he delivered the news. "Uncle, you won't believe it! There's a body in the paddy field!"

This produced a collective gasp from the listening crowd.

The man gripped the boy's arms tighter and asked, "A human body?" as the muttering around us increased and more people craned their necks to listen in.

"Yes, *yes*!" The boy tried to wriggle free. "I managed to get right up to the edge. People jostled me so much I nearly fell in myself! It's a man. I saw the trousers and shirt. Couldn't see the face though. And he's breathing mud if he's alive!"

The man cuffed him on his ear. "Watch your tongue, boy!"

A woman in the crowd called out, "What are the policemen doing?"

The boy turned towards the voice and called back, "They're just looking at the guy and talking on the phone. They might be looking for volunteers to drag the thing out, so if any of you want to be the first to see who it is, I suggest you make your way to the front!"

With that the boy managed to finally break free and run off in the direction of the town. I wondered how long it would take for the industrious fellow to pop into every shop on the main street and share his gory news.

Suddenly, the crowd surged back, and we had to move a

few feet to avoid being trampled: the body must have been pulled onto dry ground.

Turning to Vino I whispered, "I'm not an expert in forensics, but shouldn't they cordon the place off and take photographs and things?"

She elbowed me in the ribs. "This is rural Sri Lanka, not New York! You've been watching too many TV shows!"

We stopped talking as another person pushed their way out of the crowd.

"It's the English teacher at the school!" he shouted, "It's Priyanka Sir!"

I heard Vino gasp out loud this time and glanced at her. She was pale and there was a look of horror on her face. Unfortunately, I was unable to ask her anything as we were rudely pushed aside and jostled by the excited crowd. I could hear the words, "It's Priyanka Sir from the school!" pass from mouth to mouth like a tidal wave. The sound reached a crest with a wail erupting from our right. Someone was shouting, "Aiyo!"

Despite the gravity of the situation, I felt an uncontrollable urge to giggle. *This is all so surreal. Lamenting women and mysterious deaths belong in local Teledramas, not in sleepy little towns.*

I looked back at Vino, but her face was now composed, although she seemed to be grasping her bag rather tightly. I linked my arm through hers so that we did not get separated in the crowd and turned my attention back to what was being said.

"Did he drink?"

"Was he on drugs?"

"He was a respected teacher at the school, you idiot, he wouldn't have been on drugs!"

"What was he doing out here on foot? Maybe visiting some local girl?"

I felt a tug on my arm and realized that Vino was trying to leave. I followed her as she pushed her way through. The crowd had grown significantly, and the entire road was blocked by curious bystanders. In a moment's panic I realized I had no idea where we had parked our bicycles. We did not seem to be in the same place we had started, having been dragged with the shifting crowd.

"Vino!" I clutched her arm. "How do we find our bikes?"

"Let's just get to the edge of the crowd first. I think I know where we kept them."

Trusting in her sense of direction I hung on as we stumbled

around. A few minutes later I was relieved to find we had made it to our vehicles, and they were exactly as we had left them. *Perhaps, petty theft is not as common out here in the back of beyond?*

We unlocked our bikes and wheeled them towards the main road. It was almost dusk. As the adrenaline of the moment left me, my arms and legs started to protest, reminding me that I had not had this much physical exercise in years. And, we had to now cycle all the way back to the house. *So much for gradually easing my way into this new lifestyle!*

Vino was quiet as she led the way through the winding roads. She seemed to be miles away and navigating by habit. *I hope we don't find ourselves in another dead-end!* Nothing was familiar and my legs were beginning to ache. My stomach rumbled, and I realized we had not stopped for a cup of tea as originally planned. I longed for a hot bath and a snack. So, I muttered a prayer of thanks when we finally turned into Komarika Lodge.

I watched Vino as we stored out bicycles in front of the house.

"Home sweet home!"

She rewarded me with a watery smile.

Then, it dawned on me – she must have known the man

who had died! I wanted to kick myself for being so thick and insensitive. *Hadn't she jokingly mentioned a schoolteacher when I asked about her love life? Maybe, her love life was not as dull as she claimed.*

I opened my mouth to question her, but she cut me off. "I'm sorry, Kiy, I know you're curious, but I can't talk right now. We'll have a chat during dinner, ok? I think a hot bath will do me good."

I could not argue with that. "Yes," I agreed, "I feel icky and sticky all over. But, after that, I'm holding you to your promise."

Dinner was pol roti, chicken curry and sambol. Since Andy and I lived in an apartment and neither of us liked Sri Lankan curries, cooking had been quite easy. Preparing a one-pot noodle dish or pasta was a lot less time consuming than a full Sri Lankan menu. *Should I offer to make something western one evening? Would Manike be offended?* I shuddered inwardly at the thought of crossing swords with her.

I felt much better after a refreshing spell under a hot shower. It is amazing how much dust and dirt clings to you when you cycle on unpaved roads in the countryside. My muscles were still sore, and I longed to collapse into bed, but my curiosity kept me awake and alert.

I dived right in as soon as we were seated at the dining table. "So, did you know the English teacher?"

Vino glanced at the kitchen door and grimaced. I immediately understood. Manike may be listening in, and we did not want her to add to the gossip that was most likely spreading across town right now.

"Yes, a little," she replied. "The teachers all live in the town or are boarded at the school. I meet them on and off at the market, or on my rides."

"How old was he?"

"Not old. In his mid-thirties, like us."

That made me laugh. "You know, it's funny how our perspective of age changes as we grow older ourselves. When we are schooling, being twenty is old. When we start working, forty is old. When we are ready to retire, we say, 'But fifty is not that old!'"

"I hope I am young at heart even when I'm old of limb," commented Vino.

"The crowd at the paddy field sure jumped to a lot of

conclusions," I went on. "I mean, there were some wild theories, like drugs and drink, and affairs…"

"Like I said yesterday, small towns are full of nosy parkers and gossip mongers. Life is so restricted that people wait eagerly for some distraction; any distraction."

"But a dead body in a field?" I said. "Isn't that a bit much? And what happened to respecting the dead?"

"Oh, everyone is outwardly religious, but in unguarded times their real character appears. That's what we saw this afternoon. It was all so unexpected that people spoke without the usual veneer of polite society. And anyway, small town society is rarely politically correct, you know."

I digested that for a moment. There was a lot of truth in what she said.

"So, when did you take up psychology, Doctor?" I asked with a grin.

"Ha! You live by yourself in a house this size for months and see how you fare! It's either join the nosy parkers, psychoanalyze them, or run around naked with the crazies!"

That set me off. I do not think I had enjoyed myself so much in months. Our laughter brought Manike out of her domain, and the look on her face spoke volumes: she thought we were headed to an asylum. Luckily, we had finished our meal by then, so after washing up, we each took a mug of green tea to the veranda.

When we had some privacy, I tuned to Vino. "Okay. Spill."

Vino blew on the hot tea and sighed. "I met Priyanka soon after I moved here. He's a friend of our manager at the rubber plantation. He, that is, the manager, Kumar, organized a small welcoming get together for me. Not a party, just a few shorteats and mingling and so on. Priyanka was there. We immediately hit it off. He had taught at quite a few schools. And he was well-read. Friendly. We didn't go out on any dates or anything. Can you imagine going on a date in this town? I bumped into him at Eheliya one day, and we had a chat at a café. He called me a few times here at home."

I knew I should condole in some way, so, I reached for her hand and patted it clumsily as best I could. My mind raced as I hunted for something comforting to say.

"I was shocked," Vino went on, "at what those people were saying. Speculating about another person's life. By tomorrow the whole town will be convinced that he died as the result of some illicit drug deal or something! We can't even be sure it was foul play, can we?"

"You're right," I agreed. "But the police will find out what happened, won't they?"

She smiled through her tears. "Oh, Kiy! You're sweetly naive! This is a small-town police force. I'm not expecting much. It would be nice to know what he was doing out there and how he ended up in the field, but I'm not laying any large bets on it."

"Did he have any family?"

"Not that I know of."

"We'll have to find out about funeral arrangements, and so on. Maybe your manager would know?"

Vino sat up. "Yes, that's what I need. To stop wallowing, and to apply my mind to something. Helping to organize the funeral would be just the thing. Thanks, Kiy. I'll call him now."

I waited on the veranda as Vino went indoors to make her call. Mosquitoes buzzed by my ear, and I wondered if we should light a coil or burn some citronella oil. *The last thing I need is to come down with dengue fever! Maybe I should speak to Vino about that later?*

Vino had a puzzled look on her face when she joined me.

"Kumar just told me the strangest thing. Priyanka has a wife and child back in Ratnapura!"

That chased all thoughts of bugs out of my mind. "*What?* But you said…"

"I know what I said! It was what he led me to believe! He told me he was unmarried!" She collapsed into a chair and buried her head in her hands "Oh my God… *Oh, my God!*"

I dragged my chair up to hers and put my arm around her. "Is Kumar sure of this? Maybe Priyanka was divorced?"

"Oh, he's sure. He's met them! They're friends, remember!"

I took a deep breath. "Vino," I started, and then stopped. I had a lot to say but I was unsure if she was ready to hear it. "Vino, you've had a lucky escape. The guy was obviously stringing you along. He must have been looking for some excitement on the side, during term time, and going back to his family during the vacation. His sort are despicable… dogs!" My voice broke as my emotions overtook me. "I should know! Men like that are not fit to live, and you should be happy someone did him in! At least you never married the piece of shit, like I did, and found out too late!"

That produced a giggle. Her reaction was infectious, and worked up as I was, I could still see the funny side of what I had just said.

"Yes," she agreed. "In hindsight, I had a narrow escape… But teachers are supposed to be respectable."

I wiped tears of mirth off my cheeks. "Who knows, maybe the gossips in town got it right? If he could blatantly cheat on his wife and lead you down the garden path, maybe he could also be a drunk and a drug addict?"

Vino joined in with, "Maybe he had multiple affairs, and a furious lover conked him on the head!"

"Maybe he was sneaking back to his quarters and an irate husband conked him on the head!"

"Maybe an enraged mother took a broom to him!"

Our hypotheses were getting more ridiculous with every minute. But they say laughter is the best medicine, and we both felt a whole lot better afterwards.

As we giggled over our tea, I also thought about human nature. How we never really know the people we interact with. We all had our secrets, and sometimes those secrets hurt those around us.

Later, as I sank into my bed, I wondered how and why Priyanka had died. I regretted my emotional outburst. No matter how unfaithful a person had been, they did not deserve to die like that. To lie in the mud. To be the butt of everyone's speculation. To have your name sullied. I sincerely hoped Vino's prediction about the local police would prove to be false. I hoped, if it were murder, that the culprits would be brought to justice.

One thing was crystal clear: the dull and sleepy small-town had just become a whole lot more interesting.

CHAPTER FOUR

THE **SECOND DAY** of my stay at Komarika Lodge started early. This time I set my phone alarm, to ensure I did not oversleep. I may be on holiday, but that did not mean I had to laze around until mid-morning.

Breakfast was an omelette and bread. I made a mental note to drive into Eheliya and find a supermarket which sold cereals and other luxury items unavailable at the local grocery store. This led to another mental note – buy a notebook in which to write down my mental notes!

Vino reached the table just as I did.

"Good morning!"

"Morning," she replied. "Did you sleep well?"

"Oh, definitely!" I enthused. "You should run retreats! How about you?"

She pulled a face. "As well as could be hoped. Our chat helped. I don't know how I would have coped if you weren't here."

I grinned. "See, my encroaching on your hospitality has benefits for both of us!"

As we tucked into our meal, I said, "At what time does Manike come to work? For that matter, I didn't even hear her leave last night."

"She works from 7 a.m. to 7 p.m. on weekdays. I give her the weekend off."

"Erm, don't take this the wrong way, I'm not trying to dictate how you run your home or anything, but is it okay if I drive into Eheliya and buy some western food? Like cereal, for breakfast. And pasta for dinner?" I looked at her hopefully.

Vino smiled. "I understand. Believe me. Let's make a trip on Saturday and spend the day there. We can eat out. Unlike here, they even have a Cargills, Pizza Hut, KFC..."

"How could I miss Colombo with all that at Eheliya! But

seriously," I continued. "We should go. We may need to take my car to a garage after that trip, but it will be worth it!"

We were just finishing breakfast when there was a tap at the door. I raised an eyebrow. It was too early for visitors, and I did not think the neighbours dropped in for social calls. As Vino moved to answer the door I moved towards my room. I did not get far, however, before I heard a loud gasp. Two policemen were walking in followed by Vino who was looking alarmed. She showed them to the armchairs and gestured for me to join them.

"This is my friend, Kiyama Fernando. She's visiting from Colombo."

The two policemen settled in. They were both dressed in the usual khaki uniform. The older one, whom I pegged as the senior officer, was probably in his fifties with salt and pepper hair that was thin in the middle, and a pudgy face that matched his rotund appearance. The other was a lot younger. They both wore serious faces. The younger one was armed with a notebook and started writing the moment we spoke.

"What can we help you with, officer?" asked Vino, her voice shaking ever so slightly.

The senior officer began with, "My name is Inspector de Silva. We are sorry for the intrusion, but could you please give us your full name?"

"I'm Vinodhini Dias."

"Where do you work, Madam?"

"I own The Orchard Rubber Plantation. It was left to me by my uncle. I was just about to leave to oversee the office now…"

"How long have you worked there?"

"About a year." She paused. "Look, Inspector, what's this about? Has something happened at the plantation?"

"We're here about the body which was discovered in the field yesterday. Have you already heard about it?"

Vino nodded. "Oh yes, we know about that. Actually we were cycling in the area at the time and were there when they pulled it out. Why do you ask?"

He ignored her question and ploughed on. "How well did you know Priyanka Galagoda?"

This did not sound good. I did not think Vino should answer any questions without the advice of a lawyer, so, I butted in.

"Inspector, please excuse me, but why are you questioning her? She hasn't done anything wrong."

He turned and looked at me levelly. "We are speaking to

everyone who knew the victim…"

Vino and I both jumped at the word. "Victim? Was he murdered, then?"

He did not look pleased, but answered briefly, "We are dealing with it as a suspicious death. Now, Madam, if you could please answer my earlier question, how well did you know him?"

Vino swallowed nervously. I could see she was flustered but clenched my jaw to keep from interrupting again.

"I knew him through my manager, Kumar, at the rubber plantation. I met him at a function when I first moved here about a year ago. Since then, I've seen him around."

"Were you friends?"

"I wouldn't go that far… more like acquaintances."

"When did you last see him?"

"Erm… let me think… it was on Saturday." She looked at me and added, "the day before you arrived."

Inspector de Silva indicated for her to continue.

"I was cycling in town, and I stopped to talk to him. We just exchanged a few pleasantries."

There was a long silence. Vino fidgeted with her clothes,

and I wondered where this line of questioning was heading. Then the policeman said, "He died on Saturday evening or later that night."

Vino's voice was thin when she retorted, "And, what? You think *I* did it? How did he die?"

Again, he ignored her question. Instead, he asked, "Are you sure you just had a chat on the side of the road? Did you, by any chance, stop for a cup of tea at the bakery next to the grocery store?" He gave her a piercing look. "Please don't lie, Madam. Lies have a habit of being exposed… Did you have an argument?"

Vino closed her eyes. I could see that her hands were trembling. "Of course I didn't argue with him!" She took a deep breath. "Okay. We stepped into the bakery for a cup of tea since it was about four in the evening. It was a terrible cup of tea, by the way. Set you down the road to early diabetes." I winced: she was rambling. "But he was perfectly fine when I rode off!"

By this time, I was on the edge of my seat, and I could not keep quiet any longer. "How was he killed Inspector? Did someone hit him over the head? Was he poisoned? Was he stabbed?"

Annoyingly, he ignored the question, again.

"Are you sure it was a chance meeting?"

Vino glanced at me. I noticed the panic in her eyes and wondered what was happening. She crossed and re-crossed her legs but did not answer.

The policeman spoke quietly and firmly. He sounded reasonable but I noted a hint of exasperation creeping in. *Please don't let Vino's weird behaviour anger him!*

"Look, Madam, we don't want to pry into your private business, but this is an investigation into a suspicious death. If you don't cooperate now, I will have no option but to take this conversation to the station at Eheliya." He paused. "Let me ask you again. Was it a chance meeting? Please bear in mind that the victim had his phone in his pocket..." He left it at that and looked inquiringly at her, waiting for her to contribute.

Vino's shoulders slumped. She sighed and nodded. "Yes. He sent me a message asking me to meet him... But it wasn't a regular thing! There was nothing going on between us!" She almost tripped over her words as she sped on. "He has a wife and family, for heaven's sake!"

The Inspector lifted an eyebrow and nodded.

"What did you talk about?"

"Nothing important! He said he'll be going home during the school vacation. He mentioned some unruly kids in his class and how he had had to punish them last week. Just the usual stuff…" She paused and seemed to get a grip of herself. "Do you think I was the last person to see him alive?"

The Inspector nodded at his younger colleague who shut his notebook. They both stood up. "Thank you for your time, Madam. We are still tracing his final moments so I can't answer that. Please do not leave the area anytime in the near future, Madam, until this investigation is complete. We may have more questions for you as we progress. And if you think of anything new, please contact me."

He handed her a card and moved towards the door. "We'll see ourselves out."

Vino and I sat frozen in place lost in our private thoughts many minutes after the door shut behind them. I spoke first.

"Vino," I asked as gently as I could, "Are you okay?"

She nodded but I could see tears in her eyes. The interview had upset her a lot more than I had realized.

"Well! They didn't seem to be incompetent bumbling idiots who'd pin the blame onto the first person they see," I went on, hoping to lighten the mood. "I was afraid they'd be PC Plod and Company!"

Vino rewarded my effort with a small smile. "I just hope they keep an open mind. I am the newcomer to this area. It would suit a lot of people to solve this one fast and point the finger at me. I mean, *he's* a respectable member of the community. *I'm* some strange woman from Colombo!"

I frowned. She had a point. "What should we do?"

"I have to get to work," she said firmly, as she got to her feet.

"What? You're in no state to go to work! Can't they manage a day or two without you? You did say your manager was quite competent."

"But what else can I do? At least working and worrying about the business will keep my mind off this mess."

I put my hand on her shoulder. "Vino, do you trust those cops to uncover the truth?"

She looked at me, puzzled. "What do you mean?"

I struggled to put my over-worked thoughts into words. "What happens if you are the last person to see him alive? They did suggest that they found messages from you on his phone. What if they think you had an affair and then found out that he was married all along? Will they assume you killed him out of rage for fooling you?"

She pulled back and looked at me in horror. "What are you saying? Do *you* believe I killed him?" she asked in a strangled voice.

"No, no! I'm just telling you how it may look to the police. I trust everything you told me! I'm your friend, Vino. I want to help you. Here, let's sit for a second."

Once we were both off our feet, I made what is probably the most insane proposition of my life. "I think we should investigate this on our own." I held up a hand as she opened her mouth to object. "Just in case we need evidence to prove your innocence in a worst-case scenario. Waiting until after they accuse you would be too late. It's not that I don't trust them to do their jobs – it's better safe than sorry, right? We need to speak to people now, while everything is fresh in their minds. We can find out who else had a grudge against him. Although you didn't kill him, someone else did!"

She buried her face in her hands. I waited. Manike was banging pots and pans in the kitchen. A dog barked in the street outside. When she looked up, the sad, defeated look was gone. In its place was a look of fiery determination. "Yes," she said, "that's a brilliant idea! Where do we start?"

We spent the rest of the morning compiling a list of places to visit and people to talk to. Writing things down always helped me to organize my thoughts.

1) Kumar – find out more about Priyanka

2) The shops between the café and the paddy field – to trace his steps after his meeting with Vino

3) The farmer who owns the paddy field

4) Manike – for general gossip

5) The teachers at the school

6) Any other acquaintances that come up

I looked at our list feeling quite proud of the result. Put down like that the task was not as daunting as it first seemed. The only problem was that I was a complete outsider and no one in the town would be willing to talk to me. Vino, on the other hand, had at least lived here for the last year. That should carry a little more weight, but it also meant that Vino would have to take time off from the plantation. We decided to capitalize on my 'foreign' status and ask questions while pretending to do a grand tour.

We set to work immediately. I made a list of questions to ask people while Vino hammered out details with her manager over the phone.

1) When did you last see Priyanka?

2) What was he doing?

3) What was his mood like?

4) What did you speak to him about?

5) What time did he leave?

6) Do you have any ideas about who may have held a

grudge against him?

I was almost done when she rose from her seat. "So, what did he say?"

"He told me not to worry about the business, that everything is under control. I warned him that the police may turn up at his doorstep since I mentioned his name to them. He said he has nothing to hide and is more than willing to help find the killer."

"That's auspicious. Did he say anything to help us with our inquiries?"

"I asked him when he last saw Priyanka. Apparently, they haven't been in touch lately. I got a hint that Kumar knows of Priyanka's infidelities and doesn't approve. When I asked if he could think of anyone who would want to hurt him there was an awkward pause. And, then he said, no. But I don't believe him. I feel he knows something personal, but he doesn't want to speak ill of the dead."

"That's an attitude we're going to come up against repeatedly," I commented. "Let Kumar be for the moment but put him down for another call in a few days. You do need to call and check up on the business, anyway."

Vino grinned at me.

"What?"

"You sound so professional!" she said. "Like you've done this before."

"Maybe I have an innate talent for snooping? That's a career choice!" I mimed a notice board. "Kiyama Fernando – Private Investigator Extraordinaire! Andy's mother would turn in her grave. She was all stiff-upper-lip and prim-and-proper." I tried to fake a cut glass British accent. "Oh, no, my dear, that would not do at all… What would the neighbours think!"

Manike entered the hall as we laughed. She did not seem surprised to see Vino at home at this time of the morning. She must have overheard the entire interview from her post by the kitchen door. Undoubtedly, the news would be all over the town before nightfall.

"Miss Vino, since you are at home today, I thought I'll ask what you like to have for lunch?"

"Oh, the usual rice and curry would do. I'll get more vegetables from the Sunday Fair," Vino answered. I angled my head towards the cook and widened my eyes. She caught on immediately and continued with, "Manike, have you heard anything about that body which was found yesterday?"

"Hmpf! I don't know who killed him or why, but I do know Farmer Laksiri was appalled. And, I know he's going to have a hard time selling his rice, once the paddy is taken in." She sighed. "All that hard work in vain."

"Eeww!" I breathed. "I hope he destroys that part of the crop and doesn't sell it to anyone! Just imagine eating something that has been contaminated by a dead body?!"

Manike gave me a pitying look. She probably thought I was some ignorant fool from the city. "Of course he's going to get rid of that paddy! I meant the rest of the field that had nothing to do with the dead man."

Vino interrupted us. "Wait, you said you don't know who killed him. Then, everyone knows it was murder?"

"What else could it be, no? If a man takes his own life, he either shoots himself, drowns himself, or hangs himself. And usually in his own home. Not out in a stranger's paddy field!"

I realised she had omitted something. "What about poison? I thought that's the most common method used for suicide in villages?"

She gave me a hard look and I wanted to kick myself. Mental note to self – *do not point out that life in the village is inferior to that in the city!*

Manike pursed her lips primly. "Yes, life is hard for everyone. And yes, poison is easy to find in a village. But these *men*, they are the cause of all our troubles. Can't control themselves. When hard times come the weak fools can't deal with it and kill themselves. Or kill each other. And we women-folk have to bear it all up at the end."

Vino immediately jumped in. "What sorts of trouble do the men in the town get up to?"

Manike's eyes gleamed. "Well-brought-up ladies like you probably don't know the ways of men. *(I had to hide a smile at that!)* They get into all sorts of trouble, you know. There's the gambling at the Sporting Star. Wasting money on alcohol and cigarettes. Brewing illegal kasippu. Visiting those 'loose' women in Eheliya. Having a second wife on the side…"

She finally paused to take a breath, and Vino said, "That's shocking! But a teacher like Priyanka Sir wouldn't have done those things, surely?"

Manike snorted, and gave us an arch smile, which seemed to imply, 'If only you knew!'

I tried my luck. "I used to be a teacher in Colombo. The students' parents always expected the most respectable behaviour from us."

She took my bait. "Hmph! That may be in Colombo, but the teachers here are a more common lot. They are as human as everyone else."

I pretended to be shocked, and said, "But Vino Miss had met Priyanka Sir a few times and she said he was a good person!"

The floodgates opened. "Tcha! He may have taught his subject well, I don't have kids that age, so I don't know, but he was always hanging around that gambling den! And I've heard some funny stories about his liking for young girls!"

She must have seen the expression on our faces (genuine shock this time) and explained, "Oh, no, not like that! Not his students! He wasn't a pervert. That would be too much! He liked pretty girls who are just out of their teens, it seems. And I heard that he wasn't too picky about whether they were married or not!" She stopped and looked at the clock on the wall. "Tcha! Look at the time! Can't stand here gossiping all day – there'll be no food on the table!" With that, she turned and sailed into the kitchen.

Vino and I looked at each other, our eyes sparkling. We had struck gold! I had had my doubts whether she would share her gossip, but, oh boy, this little chat had opened so many new avenues that I was raring to go. I too looked at the clock. It read 11.30 a.m. We may as well leave after lunch.

"Let's move this to the veranda."

Once we were comfortable, I turned a new page in my exercise book, and wrote:

THINGS TO FIND OUT

1) Did Priyanka have a gambling addiction?
2) Was he in debt to anyone?
3) Who are his girlfriends?
4) Was he in trouble with the girls' families?

I showed this to Vino. "So, how do we find the answers?"

"I know where the Sporting Star is. Maybe we could just walk in and ask?"

"Ha! And they would just dish that information out?"

"Maybe *you* could sashay in wearing your most sexy outfit, bat your eye lashes and offer to place some bets? They probably expect all newcomers from Colombo to be wealthy and promiscuous," she said with a twinkle in her eye. "Those men will jump at the chance to make your acquaintance!"

I sniffed. "I don't want some lecherous old farts dogging my footsteps for the rest of my stay here! Anyway, I don't know the first thing about these gambling joints, and they'd realise I'm a fake the moment it came to actually placing the bets..." I paused to think. "Who were Priyanka's best friends? We could ask them in a roundabout way."

"So, that's one more thing to ask Kumar," Vino commented, as I added it to my list.

"You know, about Kumar," I said, closing my book. "I think you should be truthful and tell him you're worried about the police. Appeal to his manly sense of honour and the need to protect the weak. Tell him you fear they're going to pin this on you, and we're trying to get to the truth. He might even offer to help."

"If he does, we can send *him* undercover into the gambling den!" laughed Vino.

I pretended to consider that seriously. Then shook my head. "Nah, you may get into trouble with his wife for leading him astray. That's the last thing we need – for you to be labelled as some *'loose'* woman who wastes her money gambling and tempting men into it as well… Seriously, though, I think you need to speak with him face to face to get his sympathy. Shall we visit him tomorrow at your office?"

"Yes. That's a good idea. And I can show you around the plantation. Remember what they say about all work and no play!"

"That it makes Jill a dull girl?" I grinned. "I'm enjoying myself here, thank you, unravelling this mystery! It's giving my old brain some good exercise. I hadn't realized how stiff and staid I'd become. So, if that is the case, which is work and which is play? I'm confused!"

CHAPTER FIVE

AFTER LUNCH WE hopped on our bicycles and made our way to the scene of the crime. I was getting accustomed to the winding lanes and did not feel the distance or the time, and after what felt like minimum effort, we were overlooking the paddy fields once again.

"Okay," I said, "How do we find Farmer Laksiri?"

"Well," answered Vino. "His must be one of those houses adjoining the field. Let's just walk down. Oh, and remember to play the dumb visitor from Colombo and ask most of the questions."

I rolled my eyes and nodded. "Let's get this done."

When we reached the edge of the field, we locked our bikes and peered into the mud where the body had lain just a day ago. There was nothing to see. It was just brown oozy mud. The plants in this section of the field had been uprooted, as Manike had said. I felt a stab of sympathy for the farmer at the loss of his harvest. Paddy farmers live hand to mouth and make very little profit so an event such as this could spell disaster. If anything had fallen out of Priyanka's pockets the farmer would have found it as he cleared the spot. The curious bystanders seemed to have returned to their daily work, so our only audience was a lone scarecrow with a crazed smile on his clay pot head. It was getting hot and sticky, and although I wore a floppy sunhat and sunglasses (in keeping with the role I was playing) I yearned for an umbrella to keep off the blazing sun. We walked carefully along the bund that borders each square and crossed over to the path on the other side.

A handful of thatched huts lined the dirt road, each sharing a boundary wall with its neighbour. The walls were cracked with gashes in the fading paint. Although the huts extended inwards, only one large room was visible and broken furniture and pieces of pottery littered the doorways. Although it was past the lunch hour, the smell of rice and curry and undertones of fresh manure hung over the place. Chickens pecked industriously, hunting for seeds and worms. A goat 'baaed' at us from where he was tied to a post.

I looked at Vino. "Where do we start?"

"Let's walk around. You make a few loud comments and ask questions. Someone should appear."

Thanking my drama teacher at school I cleared my throat and said, "Oh, my, *gosh*! Is that a *goat*? I haven't seen one alive in like, *ever*! It's a lot scrawnier than I imagined. And it's nibbling on a newspaper! Ew! Reading those stories is bad enough but having it flavour your meat is just *wrong*! Oh, those chickens are just adorable! I have some salted peanuts in my bag. Do you think I could feed them?"

Vino was coughing into her sleeve. I could see tears forming in her eyes. I fanned myself and declared, "It's so *hot*! I must carry an umbrella with me next time we leave the house. Thank heavens I remembered to apply some sun block, or I'd be an ugly shade of brown by now…"

I heard a snigger behind me and turned to see a young boy of about six years of age, bare bodied except for a pair of old shorts, standing by the door of one of the huts. "Oh, hello!" I squealed. "Shouldn't you be in school at this time of day?"

Vino squatted by him. "Hi there. I'm Miss Vino from Komarika Lodge and I'm showing my friend around." She added conspiratorially, "She's never been to a paddy field… Is your mother around?"

The boy glared at us and shook his head.

"Are you alone?"

Again, he shook his head.

A figure stepped out of the gloomy house – a girl of about twenty. She, like Manike, was dressed in a floral print cheettha redi dress and had a cloth wound around her middle. "Sarath, what are you doing there?" she demanded. Her voice was high, like that of a much younger child.

"Akka, that lady was trying to poison our chickens!"

"*What*?" I shrieked. "I was *not*! I was trying to feed them!"

Vino stood up and dusted her hands. "With salted peanuts," she said pointedly. She turned to the girl inside the hut and smiled. "My friend is from Colombo and means no harm. Actually, we're just taking a stroll around the town. We heard there was some excitement here yesterday and came to see what the fuss was about."

The boy, Sarath, crossed his arms and said, "That was Priyanka Sir in the mud."

"Oh! Mud bath or mud fight?" I asked. Vino grimaced, and I realized I may be overdoing it. I shrugged.

Sarath laughed. "He was dead! Thatha said he was a menace when he was alive, and a disaster when he died!"

The girl stepped out and cuffed the boy on his head. "You watch your tongue!" She looked at us and apologized, "Please forgive him, Miss, he's a blabbermouth."

At that Sarath stuck his tongue out at her and ran off down the lane, singing,

> Sumu and Priyanka
>
> Sitting in a tree
>
> K-I-S-S-I-N-G

The girl, Sumu, grabbed a coconut husk which was lying at her feet and threw it after him. "You wait, you little rat, I'll get you for that!"

I shook my head. *Little brothers. Village or Town, North or South, nothing changed.* "Reminds me of my younger brother, years ago. Annoying little bugger, he was," I told Sumu.

"We're sorry for your loss," said Vino, "if Priyanka Sir was close to you."

The girl crossed her arms. "There was nothing between us. I don't even know what he was doing near our paddy field. Definitely not meeting me. I told him to leave me alone last week when I heard about..." She broke off, as if she had said too much.

I nudged Vino. "My friend here had a close call with him, too. Apparently, he has, or had, a wife and child in Ratnapura."

Vino glared at me, but my ploy worked. The girl's eyes lit up when she heard Vino was a victim of his charms, as well. "He was so smooth, no? And, so confident. And a good listener – I could talk for hours, and he always gave good advice." Female solidarity seemed to have loosened her tongue.

"How did you realise he was married?" Vino asked.

"I didn't know that," the girl confessed, "until you just mentioned it. My father saw him with some woman at Eheliya and was frothing mad. Thatha wanted to break his jaw for leading me on, but Amma and I convinced him to leave it alone. When I asked Priyanka, he tried to brush it off as a chance encounter, but he was a bad liar when confronted. I could see right through him, you know. I told him to sod off." Her eyes widened as she realized what she had unwittingly said about her father. "But I'm sure my father had nothing to do with his death!" she spluttered. "You've got to believe me! Anyway, they said there wasn't a mark on him, so Thatha didn't carry out his threat… Please, don't tell anyone…"

Vino laid a hand on Sumu's arm. "Your secret is safe with us. Don't worry. And I'd appreciate it if you, in turn, didn't tell anyone about my knowing him, either…"

Sumu smiled. "Deal!"

"You may have known him better than anyone else," I said, "was he angry or worried about anything the last time you spoke to him?

Sumu looked out over the paddy fields, her eyes blank. "Yes," she finally admitted, "he mentioned something about a promotion he was working for and said he didn't get it because of a teacher called Bandara Sir. He was quite angry that day. Kept insisting that Bandara Sir must have paid a bribe to become Sectional Head and that he didn't deserve it."

This girl was a fount of information! I decided to press our luck a little further. "Hey, do you know if the police found anything on him? Or if anything had fallen into the mud?"

"I don't know what they found, but I helped Thatha to pull up the paddy, and…" she broke off and looked around. I had goosebumps. *Yes! She had found something!*

"Stay here," she said and ran into the hut. When she returned, she carried a small notebook in her hand. "I found this in the mud. I haven't had the chance to clean it, so I don't know if it belonged to him. But, how else would a book get into a paddy field?"

I accepted the muddy treasure fighting the urge to dance in glee. Vino, too, looked thrilled. She clasped Sumu's hand and said, "If you hear anything more about the circumstances behind his death, can you share the information with us? We'd like to know what happened."

My elation increased when she nodded, "Sure, no problem."

We raced to our bikes and returned home in record time. I clunked mine down and dashed inside to clean the mud off the notebook. Holding it under the tap was not an option, so we took a cloth and wiped it as gently as possible. Luckily, the mud had dried and broke off easily. Also, Priyanka seemed to have favoured a ballpoint pen over ink, which was a blessing. Once the work was complete, we sat at the dining table to pour over our find.

The first dozen pages were a traditional diary cum planner, which contained quite mundane information – reminders for classes and various appointments dating back about eight months. Then, it got interesting. The pages were ruled as if for an accounts book. The notations revealed more expenses than income. Unfortunately, it did not say where the payments were going. A few such pages in, however, the trend changed. The latter half of the accounts showed a healthy balance. Large sums of money had started coming in about six months ago. Further down, there was a list of symbols which were puzzling. We could make out a circle with a bolt of lightning through it, a square with a face in the centre, a five-pointed star, among others.

I could hardly keep my excitement in check. I jabbed my pencil at the numbers and said, "I bet he had some secret scheme going. You don't get large amounts of money out of the blue!"

"It could be interest from fixed deposits," Vino suggested, playing devil's advocate.

"But wouldn't that go directly into a bank account? These look like cash payments… Ahhh!... If only we could look at his bank details!"

"We can't, so let's move one," Vino advised. "He could have participated in one of those pyramid schemes…"

"But aren't those illegal? Wait, let me Google it." I took out my phone. When I typed 'Pyramid Schemes' a flood of information appeared. "It says here, statistically about 87%

lose money. Also, each new tier funnels a percentage up the pyramid." I studied the accounts again. "But these numbers in the book show the same amount occurring each month. And there are only a few large payments coming in, that's it. I don't think it looks like a pyramid scheme. If it is not interest on a fixed deposit, and not a pyramid, what could it be?"

Vino was biting the end of her pencil. "Could he have invested in a local business?"

"Seriously? I doubt a small-town start up would give this kind of return within such a short period of time!" I stared at the numbers for a while until a new thought popped in. "Could it be blackmail?

"What?" she said, looking shocked. "Isn't that jumping to conclusions?"

"Just hear me out. There's a list of funny symbols. And look here, the same symbols appear on the side of the cash inflows. The sums are regular. This fifteen thousand rupees appears three times, with this triangular symbol on the side. This twenty thousand appears twice with this squiggly line on the side. I think he didn't want to mention names, so he wrote it in code. It has got to be blackmail!"

Vino still looked unconvinced. "Blackmail is something you read about in an Agatha Christie, not something that happens regularly in real life!"

But I was certain we were on to something. "Look, you said it the other day. There's a lot of gossip in a place like this. And I'm sure there are a lot of secrets too. People may pay a blackmailer once or twice hoping he would eventually go away. But I think human greed is such that it never stops. Then, the blackmail victim has to either inform the police, at which point their secret is no longer a secret. Or they deal with the problem in a more direct way! I think one of his blackmail victims shut him up. To solve this, all we have to do is figure out who was paying him!"

"Oh yeah, we can just carry a banner and a loudspeaker down Main Street and ask who was paying Priyanka to keep their secrets!"

Vino's sarcasm was surprising, but I dug my heels in.

"No, listen. It's not that hard. In order to blackmail someone, you have to be in a position to find out sensitive information. Priyanka was a teacher, he lived here nine months of the year. How many people did he meet regularly in this small town who had a secret to hide, and money to pay for his silence? These are large sums of money. I'm sure very few people here can afford to pay like this."

"Maybe it was lottery winning?" she ventured.

That made me laugh. "In that case, I wouldn't mind some of his good luck!" I looked at her closely. "Do you seriously think it was lottery winnings?"

"Okay…. You're right… I guess."

Vino obviously considered blackmail a very long shot. *Had living here skewed her perspective? Or have I read too many Agatha Christies?*

"Let's put blackmail at the top of our list but keep our minds open," I conceded. "Where do we start? Shall we make a list of possible suspects? 'Victims' is probably a better word for it…"

I turned a new page in my exercise book.

POSSIBLE BLACKMAIL SUSPECTS / VICTIMS

1) Other teachers
2) Business owners
3) Parents of his students

"I wonder why he needed so much cash in a hurry?" I pondered aloud.

"Perhaps it was for a family emergency, like a sudden illness? Or it could be gambling debts. We should ask Kumar tomorrow."

I flipped through Priyanka's notebook to the end. There

was a folded sheet of paper at the back. I extracted it gingerly and spread it out on the table. It was a letter.

"Look at this," I breathed.

The very top and bottom were in tatters where the mud and water had damaged the paper. So, there was no date or signature. It read,

Priyanka,

I was surprised to hear you are teaching at the local school. We should meet up for a drink sometime. I will be in town…

"It sounds like someone was visiting. But it's difficult to say when. Could be fairly recently or years ago!"

"The letter must have had some value, or he wouldn't have kept it," said Vino.

"Maybe he was meeting an old girlfriend," I suggested. "Hey! What if he had an affair with someone in Ratnapura or Eheliya… some rich married woman… and he blackmailed her too?"

"But meeting a woman for a drink?" Vino sounded sceptical. "This is not Colombo. There are no restaurants or trendy pubs at every street corner. He lived at the school. He couldn't have taken a woman there. He would have had to buy a bottle from the Wine Stores and meet his friend at someone's house. Not the ideal way to meet an old flame for blackmail or to resume an affair!"

I laughed. "You seem to have got over your shock and disappointment."

"Definitely. I'm leaning towards disgusted, now. Who would have known he was such a criminal and a creep!"

I patted her arm. "I understand the sentiment," I said with feeling. "So, it could have been a jilted lover… It needn't be a woman at all, you know…"

Vino looked horrified. "I cannot imagine Priyanka having an affair with a *man*!"

"No! Not what I meant… He could have met a man for a drink!"

"Same problem. Where?"

"The gambling den?"

She shrugged. "Sounds like we have our work cut out for us. Kumar might shed some light tomorrow." She stood up and stretched. "I'm feeling cross-eyed looking at these symbols and numbers and my head's woozy from all the theories! Let's take a break."

The next morning, we cycled to The Orchard Rubber Plantation for our meeting with Kumar. It took almost half an hour to get there – no wonder Vino was in such good shape! Surprisingly, I enjoyed the journey. We left early to avoid the midday heat. The roads were lined in trees and a steady breeze ruffled my hair. We passed through the town and turned down multiple little lanes bordering rubber estates. The trees were slender with a silvery grey bark. I let my imagination take flight as I pumped my legs. *What would these groves look like on a moonlit night? Would the silvery trees reflect the light? Would wood nymphs emerge and dance to a ghostly tune? Perhaps we could ride this way on the next Poya day. Maybe we could have a late-night picnic?* I spotted a small brook running along the roadside, and idly wondered if any harvest mice scamper by when no one is around to document their movements…

I reigned in my rambling thoughts as we reached the entrance to the plantation. A nondescript wooden gate opened to yet another dirt path which wound up a small hill. By now my legs were demanding a break, so I dismounted and wheeled the bike the last few yards. The plantation offices were in an old bungalow. At first glance it looked like any other residence but a closer look revealed air conditioner units and satellite dishes that clashed with the architecture.

We locked our bikes and I followed Vino as she led the way

to her office.

The interior had been recently renovated and, although I am no expert, I could see they had upgraded the amenities while preserving the style of the original building. The walls were painted in bright colours, and potted plants and modern furniture gave the place a professional look. Vino's office was not large and retained the old teak furniture I expected to see in a building such as this. I recognized a beautiful crystal vase and asked, "Wasn't this in your apartment in Colombo?"

"Yes, it was. You have a great memory," Vino said. "When I realised that I'd have to live here if I accepted my uncle's bequest, I brought my little treasures with me."

"Nice. And the furniture?"

"That set is from Komarika Lodge. You wouldn't believe how cluttered it was when I moved in. My first job was to play interior designer, which was a lot of fun, actually."

I took a seat in a comfortable armchair as Vino called Kumar to join us. He shook hands with me as soon as he entered and took the last armchair in the room. Kumar looked exactly as I expected: around forty years of age, going bald, bespectacled, and round about the middle. He looked good humoured and relaxed, which boded well for our inquiry. He was in a light blue shirt without a tie, and dark trousers: the quintessential office look.

"Hello, Kiyama. Vinodhini mentioned you many times over the past few days. It's a pleasure to finally meet you."

"Likewise," I responded. He had a strong grip, and I was pleased to note he did not present a limp hand to ladies, as was the usual custom.

"So, what have you two ladies got yourselves into?" he inquired, once we were all seated.

Vino and I exchanged glances. "We haven't got ourselves into anything," she replied. "Why do you ask?"

"It's just that the policemen who called on me asked an awful lot of questions about you and Priyanka. I didn't know you two were that well acquainted."

"Acquaintances is exactly what we were," Vino replied firmly, "although the cops believe otherwise. And this is why we want to speak to you so urgently. The police think I killed Priyanka!"

Kumar looked startled.

"Yes, that's why we need your help. We have to get to the bottom of this before I'm carted off to jail for a crime I didn't commit." She looked at him steadily. "Kumar, were you able to find out how Priyanka died?"

It was my turn to look startled.

"I told him to ask the policemen if he got the chance," she explained with a shrug.

Kumar nodded. "Yes, I asked them. And they said he was poisoned. Some insecticide with a long name. That's the most common method for murder and suicide among farming communities so he could have been killed by anyone."

Vino grimaced. "Well, at least we know the cause of death. I guess anyone could have slipped it into his drink?"

"I assume it tastes horrible. You'd need something with a really strong flavour to mask the taste!" I commented.

"Regardless, taking poison is the poor man's answer to a lot of problems," Kumar remarked.

I had a question of my own. "You knew Priyanka and his family. Vino didn't even know he had a family until you mentioned it the other day. We need more information if we are to solve this."

"Of course," he said. "What do you need to know?"

"How did you know him?"

"We were batchmates at uni together. You know how it is. We became good friends when we were ragged as Freshers. We kept in touch on and off over the years. I was surprised to find out that he was teaching here. He was always the ambitious sort. But I guess sometimes things don't work out the way you want."

"Did he have any financial difficulties?"

Kumar frowned. "Teachers don't get paid a lot, and we can all do with a little more these days. But, no, he didn't mention anything to me."

"What about his family? Did they need any money in a rush, for any emergency?"

"No."

"Do you know if he liked to gamble?"

Kumar looked uncomfortable, but Vino took over. "I know he was your friend, and you don't want to say anything against him, but we need to know. You see, we found a notebook belonging to him and there were some odd accounts in it. He was spending large amounts of money. If it was gambling, then that opens up a whole list of suspects."

I thought Vino sounded convincing and was doing well.

Kumar obviously thought so too since he caved in and said, "Okay. I'll share what I know, but it must not leave this room. Yes. He liked to gamble on and off. His wife asked me to keep an eye on him, but I don't live in town, and he lodges at the school, so there wasn't much I could do. I knew he met some friends down at the Sporting Star, but I didn't know it was a big problem!"

"There were a lot of things about him that both of you didn't know," I said, joining the conversation. "The impression I've got so far is that he was smooth and an opportunist. He seemed to have lived a double life. I mean look at the things we've learned!"

"Double life!" Kumar blurted. "What?"

Vino sighed. "I didn't want to give you all the gory details, but, since Kiy has let the cat out of the bag…" She paused, and then rattled off. "We met a girl who said she had an affair with him but broke it off when she realized he had more than one girlfriend. His notebook has accounts of large amounts of money coming in and going out, and we suspect gambling debts and blackmail."

I watched Kumar carefully as Vino dropped this bombshell. He looked appropriately shell-shocked.

"We hate to tarnish the memory of your friend…," I started, but Kumar rose to his feet. He looked agitated and did not let me finish.

"You got that right! You are dragging his good name through the mud with these stories! Priyanka was a respectable man. He was a teacher!" He moved towards the door.

But Vino had Priyanka's notebook in her hand, and she held it out to him. "This is the book the farmer found where he died. Here, take a look, and see what conclusions you come to. Maybe we got it wrong."

The need to check the evidence was too much for Kumar and he grabbed the book. We waited patiently while he studied it. Finally, he looked at us in disbelief. "If I hadn't seen it with my own eyes…"

"Do you think it's blackmail?" I asked.

His shoulder slumped as he nodded. "It looks like it."

We contemplated the implications of that in silence.

"We didn't speak much over the last few months. I put it down to work pressure. He was teaching the O' Level students and preparing kids at that level is stressful. I didn't think he was avoiding me."

"Speaking of which, did he have any rivals in school?" I asked, remembering Sumu's story.

"He was hoping for a promotion and working hard to get it. He was tutoring weaker students after school and trying some new things in his classes to motivate them. I don't know if he was successful."

"We heard that he didn't get the promotion, and that he was quite mad at a Bandara Sir who was appointed Sectional Head, but Priyanka claimed he had achieved it through underhand methods. Maybe he bribed the principal?" I speculated. And, then I sat up. "Could that have been the start of his blackmail? I mean, maybe he had evidence of bribery and decided to make Bandara pay. And, once he realized how lucrative it was maybe he found other victims."

I turned to Kumar. "Do you know any of his work colleagues? Could you introduce us to someone?"

"My children are still in the Primary. Priyanka taught the upper school."

Vino suddenly clapped me on my arm. "I know! Why don't you join the staff as a temporary English teacher? You have the necessary background; you can work undercover!"

I groaned. "Are we back to the entire undercover thing?" I raised my eyebrows at Kumar. "She made me play the stupid tourist. Then, she wanted me to gamble, which I refused. Now this!"

Kumar laughed. "Vinodhini can be very convincing. I should know! If you were a teacher in Colombo, then offering to help out for the rest of the term may be a good way of getting to know the staff as well as the workings of the school."

"But I don't know the syllabus!" I protested.

Vino brushed that away. "Oh, don't worry. You're a qualified literature teacher. They need a general English teacher. It'll be a cakewalk. And you know the government syllabus can't be that bad!"

"But I hate wearing saree!" I whined. "I don't even own one! I'm sure a government school has very strict regulations on attire!"

I could see Kumar laughing to himself. We must sound like a comedy act!

"I have a few that you can borrow. And maybe we can ask them to bend the rules for a temporary position. Come on, Kiy, you know you want to do this!" Vino was not ready to give up. "And you can't live on the interest of your fixed deposits forever. You need a job. This won't pay much, but two for the price of one is a killer deal…"

I almost choked. "Killer being the operative word here!"

"That's settled then. Kumar, can you introduce us to the principal? Maybe tell her that you've found a teacher to take over Priyanka's duties?"

He seemed a little reluctant but agreed.

"Thank you so much," Vino said. "You're a life saver!"

"We'll see about that," I muttered. "I may break my neck tripping over a saree. Wouldn't be much of a life saver then!"

Vino leaned towards Kumar and whispered, "Just ignore her! Besides, our next assignment is to infiltrate his gambling den and neither of us can go undercover there. We were hoping you'd do it!"

Kumar's eyes widened in alarm, and he jumped out of his seat.

"I'll go and make that appointment with the school principal right now," he said, and bolted out of the room.

Vino and I spent the rest of the morning touring the plantation. The Orchard Plantation collected the rubber sap from the trees and supplied it to independent factories. The factories turned the white goo into the rubber we use daily. Having lived in Sri Lanka all my life, I had learned about the process in school. I also had a vague memory of visiting a plantation during a school educational trip in the past. But if they ever taught us the ins and outs of this industry, that knowledge was lost to time.

Walking around thousands of trees was a refreshing change from sleuthing. Vino explained how the trees need to be planted at even distances from each other and how the bark needs to be scored in order to collect the sap. This is called rubber tapping. The cups which collect the sap are hardly visible from afar. The tracks cut into the bark have a symmetrical beauty. But I was feeling morbid, and the trees looked like upright patients in white hospital gowns, donating their life blood for the benefit of others. My skin crawled when Vino offered to show me some of the plantation workers slicing the bark, and I refused. Watching someone drag a hooked knife across the white skin of the tree would, I was sure, give me nightmares. I didn't voice my thoughts, though, and suggested that we make our way home for lunch.

Neither of us knew then, that the events of the coming afternoon would test our friendship.

CHAPTER SIX

AFTER LUNCH, Vino dragged me to her bedroom and pulled out some of her sarees. She favoured cottons in pastel shades. I took one blouse into my hands and remarked, "No way am I going to fit into this!" I demonstrated by poking my arm through the sleeve – I was able to wear it only up to my elbow.

She grabbed it from me and turning it inside out inspected the lining. "No problem. There's over an inch here. We can let it out. Your arms aren't that flabby!"

I pulled a face. "I hate sewing!"

"Well," said Vino firmly, "you can either handle the sewing machine, or pick out the old line, but we are going to share the work."

I do not react well to authority, and I do not like being told what to do. And something that really gets under my skin is being forced to do something I would rather avoid. This was something I would definitely avoid. I hated sarees and sewing, and Vino's tone of voice was not helping.

"Why don't *you* take up teaching? Use that tone of voice with a class and they'll be hopping through hoops in no time! And, besides, shall we at least wait until we know I've got the job? There's no point giving myself a headache peering at tiny stitches if I'm not going to wear the darned thing!"

"None of these clothes are darned, thank you very much," laughed Vino. I knew she was trying to defuse the situation, but I was angry now and I lashed out.

"Do you know why I married a foreigner? Because there are some aspects of our Suddha Sinhala culture that I don't like. Being forced to encase yourself in six yards of cloth is one. I'd much rather be wrapped in a shroud!" I collected myself with difficulty and stormed out of the room before I said something that I would regret. I ran into my room and slammed the door. I dearly wanted to throw something but resorted to punching the pillows instead.

I grabbed my latest read off the bedside cupboard and tried to immerse myself in the story. Having battled with my temper all my life, I know that losing myself in a book is the only way to calm down and forget my troubles. Luckily, Vino gave me some space and the tap at the door came half an hour later. I opened the door sheepishly.

"I'm so sorry, Vino," I started before she could have her say. "You've been so kind to take me in. I really need to keep my temper in check."

She gestured for me to stop. "It's okay, Kiy. I shouldn't have been so bossy. Being on your own can do that. I know I tend to steamroll over everyone else."

"Truce?" I asked.

"Truce," she replied. "By the way," she said as she led the way back to her room. "I totally understand how you feel about sarees. I don't wear them either!"

I laughed.

"And I promise not to wrap you up in one against your wishes. You don't have to take the job at the school. We can find some other way…"

"No," I broke in. "I want to help you. And I'm curious now. I want to know what happened to Priyanka. If I need to wear a saree to solve this mystery, then that's what I'm going to do.

Oh, and by the way," I added as we sat down. "I hope you have a lot of pins!"

As we sorted the clothes we had pulled out of her wardrobe, I commented, "Kumar was reluctant to divulge any juicy titbits about his friend's life."

"Hm, I was surprised that he volunteered as much as he did. He's a nice guy but quite strait-laced. To be honest, I'm surprised he was friends with Priyanka at all. I guess Priyanka was able to pull the wool over everyone's eyes – not just the ladies'."

"There's no way he's going into the Sporting Star to get us more information!"

Vino giggled. It was a rather humorous image. Geeky Kumar would stick out like a sore thumb.

"I've been thinking about that," she said. "The accounts show that he was able to pay back most of what he owed. So, there's no reason why one of his gambling colleagues, or a loan shark, would want him dead."

As she spoke a whole new scenario jumped into my head. "What if he saw someone else whom he knew. Someone respectable who wanted to hide his gambling habit. What if he blackmailed that person? Or here's another one, what if the loan shark figured out that the money came from illegal means and tried to blackmail Priyanka in turn?"

Vino groaned. "You're giving me a headache!"

"But both those are possible! We have to find out who runs the gambling joints and who lends money in this town, apart from the banks."

Vino stood. "There's only one person we know who can tell us that. Manike."

Manike was drinking a cup of tea in the back yard. She looked surprised to see us there. "Vino Miss!" she exclaimed. "Are you looking for something?"

"Yes," Vino smiled. "We are. And you're the only person who can help us."

Looking gratified, Manike smiled back. "Yes, Miss?"

"We need to know who owns the Sporting Star and who lends money in town. Not the banks. Someone who would provide money in an emergency without all the red tape and forms."

"Miss! Are you in any trouble?" she gasped.

"No, no. Don't worry. We just want to speak to the guy."

Manike looked unconvinced. "Those people are dangerous. They're involved in a lot of criminal activities. A well-bred lady like you can't just walk in and talk to them!" Then, with a gossip's instinct, she asked, "Does this have anything to do with Priyanka Sir's death?"

"Everything that happens these days seems to be related to his death," I commented.

"Manike, shall I let you in on a secret?" Vino asked, taking a seat nearby. "You saw those policemen visit the other day. Well, they think I killed Priyanka Sir! Can you believe that? So, we're trying to figure out who killed him to prove that I'm innocent. We need to know about his gambling. You will help us, won't you?"

Manike looked pleased that Vino had shared this piece of news with her. I hoped the gossip would not reach the ears of the policemen in turn. That would put a spoke in our wheels.

"Tell you what, Miss. My son, Siril, knows the man you need. His name is Ariyawansa. He owns the Sporting Star, and he also gives loans on the side. If you ask me, he behaves like a gentleman but it's all an act. I'll ask Siril to come here this evening. It's best if you take a man with you, no, just in case. Two beautiful, wealthy young ladies like you should not walk around at night, unattended. Keep Siril with you during the entire interview, also. I'll tell him not to let you out of his sight until you are safe back in this house."

"Manike, you are a genius!" exclaimed Vino. "We knew you would solve our problem!"

Manike beamed.

The hours until evening dragged by like a car on three wheels. Vino and I occupied ourselves by doing little mundane tasks around the house. More than once, I caught myself reading through my book of notes. I was so wound up by the impending adventure that I even helped her to adjust one of the hated saree blouses to fit my size!

Finally, Manike stepped into the living room and informed us her son was waiting in the veranda. We grabbed our handbags and all but rushed out. Siril was small-made, dark, and thin, very unlike his mother. He had inherited her teeth, though. He reminded me of a ferret when he regarded us nervously. He looked more likely to bolt down a hole than defend us in times of danger. I hoped his mother had briefed him on this evening's duty. Manike laid my doubts to rest by launching into a lengthy set of instructions on what he was to do. If he followed them to the letter, he would be a shadow stuck to our side. I was impressed by her authority and tone. Obviously, she was the matriarch in her family and not to be crossed.

Once she was done, Vino stepped out. "No need to worry. I'm sure everything will be okay. Shall we go in the car?"

Siril's eyes lit up and I assumed very rarely did such an invitation come his way. Vino got into the passenger seat, and I instructed him to climb in at the back. Soon, we were on our way.

The money lender's building was above a cell phone repair shop on Main Street. It was the type of place you would not look at twice. Even though it was almost six o'clock, the shop downstairs looked busy with customers walking in and out every few minutes. Siril informed us that this was the only such shop in the area and since everyone now owned a cell phone, maintenance was high priority. He led us round to the back where a simple iron staircase took us up. The door was also metal and was decorated in scratches and dents. Siril knocked twice. The door was immediately opened by a large, bearded man wearing a vest and sarong and smelling strongly of stale sweat.

"What is it?" he barked.

Siril flinched and said, "I have some visitors for Mr. Ariyawansa."

The guard eyed us up and down, a slow smile appearing on his face as his gaze lingered on my chest. I fought the urge to cross my arms in front of me.

"Really? And do they have an appointment?"

"No…" spluttered Siril.

The guard made as if to shut the door, so I stuck my hand out. "Wait! We can make it worth his time. Why don't you check with him first before you slam the door! Tell him it's about Priyanka!"

My voice was a lot higher than normal. I hoped the man did not realise how nervous I was.

He stared at me for a few seconds and nodded. "Stay here," he growled as he turned and disappeared.

Feeling a little like a dog ordered to sit, I leaned against the railing. Vino dragged me back, saying, "Better not do that. It looks like it may collapse any minute."

"Charming joint," I told Siril as the minutes ticked by.

A gentle breeze ruffled my hair.

Being above ground level afforded us a nice view of the town and adjoining fields. The evening was muggy hinting at rain. I hoped it would not pour until after we got back home. It was so quiet, compared to Colombo. There were no buses tearing down the road every few seconds. No blare of horns. No shouts of laughter. Only the occasional solitary vehicle making its way quietly down the road. It was hard to imagine any form of crime in such a calm setting. But here we were, waiting to be led into the lion's den.

The silence was broken by the shriek of metal as the door opened wider. The guard gestured for us to follow him.

My throat felt dry. I looked at Vino, and stepped in.

The interior was dimly lit. The room stank of cigarette smoke, alcohol, and bodily fluids. I wanted to gag. Some old furniture that looked as if they had been rescued from a dumpster lined the walls. I could see some bottles of alcohol scattered on a table on the far side. In the centre of the room was a pool table. Four scruffy looking youth who were playing a game stopped and leered at us as we walked by. The room was so small that there was barely enough room for us to edge around them. The boy nearest to me moved his playing arm back as I passed so that he elbowed me in the stomach. I fought the urge to shove him back and kept walking until we entered an inner room.

This was better maintained and set to look like an office. A large desk took pride of place. Behind it sat Mr. Ariyawansa. There were no chairs on our side, so we were forced to remain standing. At first glance, the money lender looked like any successful local businessman. His hair was neatly cut. He wore a moustache favoured by Kollywood actors from India. A thick gold chain glinted over a dark shirt. I could also see many gold rings on his stubby fingers. He steepled those fingers and asked, "Who do I have the pleasure of meeting?" His voice had the rasp of a serious smoker.

Vino stepped forward and introduced herself as the owner of a local rubber plantation, and me as a visitor from Colombo.

"And, of course, I know Siril. Doesn't his mother work for you?"

I swallowed hard. The last thing we needed was for these men to know where we lived. Vino ignored the question and continued. "We know that Priyanka owed you some money. I'm a friend of the family and I didn't want his wife to learn about his activities the hard way. Did he owe you anything when he died?"

Mr. Ariyawansa smiled, showing crooked teeth. "So, you're here on behalf of the widow?"

"Yes."

He regarded us for a few seconds and said, "No. His debts were all paid."

I took this as my cue to join in. "That's a relief to hear. But it's weird that a government teacher on such a meagre salary could have paid everything off like that."

"I don't ask them where the money comes from as long as it fills my pockets."

"But you are such a knowledgeable man of the world. Surely, you must have some suspicion."

He smiled and asked, "Is this information also for the grieving widow?"

"No," I admitted. "This is for our own curiosity."

Vino jumped in. "Well, it is partly for the widow too! We don't want any nasty rumours to reach her ears about anything illegal Priyanka may have done to get rich quick!"

He laughed. "You two should have got your stories straight before walking in. I will tell you this much. I neither know, or care, where my debtors get the money. They can rob a bank for all I care. And I don't deal in blackmail."

He must have seen something in our faces at the mention of the word since he nodded and continued, "Yes, I can guess what you're fishing for." He stood, hands on hips. "And now, as I recall, you promised to make it worth my while to see you."

"How much?" I said as I clutched my bag, praying that he named a reasonable amount.

He walked around the table and stood before us. I felt awkward and uncomfortable. The room was getting claustrophobic with five people standing around. I could not step left, right, backward, or forwards without bumping into someone. Vino, too, felt tense next to me.

"Oh, I have enough money. A few thousand more won't make a difference. What I want is…" His words were drowned out by a loud banging on the front door.

"Police! Open up!"

Vino and I shared a look of panic. *What would the police think when they found us here?*

Ordering us to stay put, Ariyawansa and his henchman left to deal with the problem. The voices were outside. Obviously, the police had not forced their way in, yet. With the recreation room between us and the door, we heard only snatches of conversation. I was sure I heard the name 'Priyanka'. The police must be following up on his gambling debts just as we were. How I would love to see their faces when they realise all his debts had been paid off!

I nudged Vino and whispered, "We have the upper hand because we have his notebook!"

Siril was cowering behind the door, a look of fear in his eyes. I wondered what he did for a living. No honest man would be so afraid of the local police. I gestured to catch his attention and asked, "Is there any other way out of here?"

He shook his head, not daring to speak.

"There must be a way! A man like Ariyawansa wouldn't set up office in a room with only one exit!"

Vino shushed me as the front door shut. We heard footsteps approaching. To our relief only Ariyawansa entered the room. He resumed his seat behind the desk and asked, "Do the police know you are nosing around?"

Vino and I shared a glance but did not reply.

"You don't have to answer. I will contact you at some later date with regards to payment for services rendered today. I did not tell the police why you were here, but they know two ladies in western dress are in the building. You will most probably meet them on your way out..."

He made a dismissive gesture and opened a file on his desk. We took the hint and left as fast as we could.

My heart was hammering in my chest. I felt lightheaded.

Would the police be waiting to arrest us outside? Having a creep like Ariyawansa refuse to talk about us only made things look worse. I glanced at Siril who was just behind us as we descended the staircase outside. *Would being found in his company be a black mark against us?*

Sure enough, as we turned back into Main Street two torches flashed in our faces. I heard a yelp behind me and saw Siril backing against a wall. Darkness had fallen while we were inside, and the light blinded me. I could not see who was there but had to assume the worst. I felt Vino grasp my hand as we stopped walking. I raised an arm against the glare and asked, "Who's there?"

"Ladies," said an indistinct voice, "Were you at Ariyawansa's place just now?"

I gulped. Deciding a lie would land us in more hot water I answered in the affirmative. The torches were lowered. Blinking in the sudden darkness, I peered at the forms of two men standing by the road. They looked awfully familiar. I felt Vino tighten her grip on my fingers as we walked forward.

"And what would two respectable ladies be doing in that den of thieves?" asked Inspector de Silva.

I sighed. "Look, Inspector, we got lost and went up the wrong staircase. Vino here insisted it was wrong, but I was pig-headed and dragged her along. I was looking for…" and I stopped, faking a cough. *I had not thought this through! What could I possibly have been looking for above a cell phone repair shop?*

"She was looking for a place to fix her laptop. It made sense that that would be above a place that repairs phones!" Luckily, Vino was much quicker on her feet that I was.

"Yes!" I agreed enthusiastically. "The battery on my laptop is wonky and I need to complete some important work and I need to get it fixed ASAP…" I trailed off as I realized I was rambling.

Inspector de Silva did not look convinced. "Then why did Ariyawansa hint that you had important business with him?"

"Oh, was it you at the door?" I asked brightly, trying to buy some time. "How can we possibly know why a man like that does whatever he does? Honestly, I still can't believe that doorman let us in! Must have been a fluke!"

Inspector de Silva's voice hardened as he said, "Do you expect me to believe that the two of you waltzed into that room while looking for a computer repair shop? Please! Give me some credit! I know you are from Colombo, and you probably have little respect for policemen but don't insult my intelligence! What were you really doing there?"

I froze in his glare. Luckily, we were distracted by a loud

crash behind us. I spun around to see that Siril had knocked over an aluminium bucket that had been by the wall. That focused the Inspector's attention on our companion.

"And what are you doing with him? He's a sneak thief!"

I heard Vino gasp by my side. "He's my cook's son. We needed someone to guide us around and she sent him…" She trailed off as the policeman stared at her. Suddenly, he began to laugh.

"You two are amateurs. You've been brought up to be truthful and make a mess when you are required to lie. Okay. I will not arrest you today. But please, choose your acquaintances and guides more carefully."

I wanted to sit on the dirt floor. I was so relieved.

"And," he went on, "I suspect this has something to do with that teacher's death. If I find you meddling in police business, I will not be this lenient. Understood?"

Feeling like a child chastised by a headmaster, I nodded.

Just then, a green BMW stopped by the side of the road, and a man got out. Clean shaven, dressed in linen pants, button down shirt and loafers, he looked oddly out of place in the middle of a small town. He walked up to us and said, "Ladies, are you stranded? Or lost? Can I be of assistance?" He spoke with a faint British accent.

Vino, the two policemen, and I stared at him in surprise. I glanced at Vino, who shrugged. The newcomer sensed our astonishment and said, "Oh, I'm sorry. I may have misinterpreted the situation. I thought you were asking for directions."

That was too much for me. All the tension I had been holding in broke forth like a dam, and I started giggling. It was now their turn to look at me. I held up a hand as I tried to control myself. "Please, ignore me! It's just that… after everything that has happened today… I realized that I'm very much lost and in need of directions… metaphorically speaking!"

The Inspector shook his head and turned to leave. "I hope I don't see you again."

Soon, it was just Mr-BMW, Vino and I left standing by the side of the road. Siril was nowhere to be seen. The arrival of the police had scared him off. I pitied him. His mother would not be pleased to hear he had abandoned us in the dark on Main Street.

"I'm Kiyama and this is Vinodhini," I said as I shook hands with our would-be-saviour. "It was very nice of you to offer to help but we found what we were looking for, and then the police found us… I'm sorry, that sounds like we were up to no good. Nothing like that…"

Vino came to my rescue. "That's Kiyama's car right there. We were just about to leave."

"I'm Trehan. I live in that monstrous old house just out of town. Do you live here? Or are you on holiday?"

Vino jerked a thumb at me. "She is. I live here."

"Really? That's great! I just inherited that house. You may have already heard about this… but… I'm renovating it and turning it into a hotel. I don't want to sound like a snob, but I had grave doubts as to whether I'd find anyone I could relate to here. The past few months have not been pleasant: no company, you see. I lived most of my life in the UK and I feel like a fish out of water amidst the farmers and local businessmen. The hotel will be ready soon and I was compiling a list of locals I could invite for the opening, but…"

"Oh well, we're also just ordinary, hard-working folk," Vino interrupted him, heading towards my car. "And we need to get home before it gets too late rather than hang around on the streets like this."

Trehan laughed. "Oh, I'm not cruising the streets looking for some action! I was in Colombo the whole day on business and just drove back." He paused, looking a little awkward. "Erm, listen, can I invite you both over to my place sometime for a meal? I need to get some feedback on the changes I'm making, the restaurant ideas and so on from someone who has been to a boutique hotel. And I'm sure a female touch would work wonders too!"

Vino didn't sound too keen but that sounded like fun. It would ease the boredom of my stay. "Sure, why not?" I agreed. "I'm not an authority on the hospitality industry or interior design, but I'd love to see the place. The building looks impressive from afar." I handed him a visiting card. "That's my number. Give me a ring sometime. Vino and I would both like to check it out."

As we drove back home Vino commented, "You hit it off well with him."

"Oh, don't read too much into it. I was just happy to have something else to do while you're at work. And we can't be investigating this twenty-four seven. Giving feedback on a new hotel could be just the thing I need. And you're the one who was yearning for some time at the spa, remember? What better way to get an invitation than to make friends with the owner himself?"

I could see her smiling. "What?" I asked, as I turned in at the gate.

"It just occurred to me that he's your type," she said, with a smirk.

"Oh, and what type is that?"

"Lived abroad. Well-travelled. Well-dressed. Polite. Need I go on?"

"Even if he is, what's your point?"

"Oh, come on, Kiy! You know what I'm getting at! A little holiday romance wouldn't hurt!"

I blushed. "I'm still married," I reminded her.

"Almost separated and heading for divorce," she reminded me. "You should take this opportunity to consider your options. You know, decide whether you want to give it another chance with Andy, or whether you want to start seeing other people. No pressure. Just have fun!"

"Yeah, no pressure at all," I muttered as we entered the house.

CHAPTER SEVEN

I **POTTERED AROUND** the house the next morning. After the excitement of the previous night I found it difficult to set my mind to anything. Vino had gone to work saying she needed to check on things and would be back for lunch as usual. I avoided the kitchen since I did not want to discuss our evening's escapade with Manike. Curiously, she did not badger me with questions either. Perhaps her son's behaviour had left her embarrassed. She had promised that he would bring us safely home. I wondered whether she knew about his reputation with the police.

I sat at my laptop and used Google Earth to find the large

mansion on the outskirts of the town. It was located atop a small hill overlooking the paddy fields and seemed an ideal spot for a hotel. I let my mind wander as I imagined tourists cycling past the greenery, enjoying boating excursions in the nearby river, sampling the local cuisine, learning to cook with home cooks in the area, and sitting with a glass of wine in the evening by a sparkling pool. Hmm... it definitely had potential.

My daydream was interrupted by the ringing of my phone: it was Vino.

"Hey, how are things going?" I asked.

"Quite good. The place is working like clockwork. Listen, I called because Kumar has got us an appointment to meet the principal of the school this afternoon. I thought I'd give you a heads up and time to prepare."

The school! I had completely forgotten about the teaching post!

"Yeah, sure. Any idea what he said about me?"

"Only that you are a friend of a friend who's on holiday for a few weeks, and that you used to teach in Colombo. The principal is a lady called Mrs. Palpola. She said she will speak to you and see. Let's discuss what we're going to say when I come for lunch, okay?"

After I hung up, I Googled the Government Education

Department and looked up the current English language syllabus. It did not look tough to teach. I knew many children living outside the large commercial cities used very little English in their daily lives. Teaching the subject in that environment would be a challenge. I made a face. This was why I opted to teach English literature to international school students in Colombo, rather than general English in the outskirts. But it was all for a good cause. And the teaching post would be temporary.

I took out my exercise book and made a list of questions.

1) Which grades would I need to teach?
2) What are the working hours like?
3) How long would I need to fill the post?
4) How many students are there in a class?
5) Do I need to wear saree to work?

I decided that negotiating a salary was not worth the effort since full time teachers are paid a paltry amount to begin with. I would take whatever was offered for my part time work and count it as pocket money.

My research was done, and I was as ready as I would ever be by the time Vino returned. At about 1 p.m. we left the house in my car – neither of us wanted to be hot and sweaty as we faced a job interview. And, no, I did not wear a saree. Instead, I wore the only conservative blouse and pants I had packed. I decided it would be better to show the principal who I am from the outset, so that there would be no misunderstandings.

Kumar joined us at the entrance. The building had no character, in my opinion. It was just a large block of weather-beaten, faded white. If a building could look jaded, then this was it. The signage proclaimed PARKADUWA CENTRAL COLLEGE in large letters; the very same sign Vino had pointed out to me during our bicycle tour of the town a few days ago. Who would have guessed at the time that I would be applying for a job?

Reflecting on the vagaries of the world, I followed Kumar in. It looked like a burrow with corridors zigzagging in all directions. Multiple staircases climbed up to the first floor. There were a few students loitering nearby, backpacks on the ground. They were all in the standard white uniform one associates with local schools in Sri Lanka. The girls wore their hair in two plaits tied with a dark blue ribbon at the ends. Uniform black shoes and white socks completed the look. That did not bode well for my campaign to avoid wearing a saree to work. This place looked very prim and proper, and I entered the Principal's Office with feelings of antipathy clouding my mind.

We were shown straight in. The principal Mrs. Palpola was seated behind a desk. She was middle-aged, dressed in a purple saree, with her hair in a neat bun. She greeted us with a welcoming smile and gestured for us to be seated.

"How are you, Mr. Padmasiri?" she asked as we made ourselves comfortable.

"I'm doing well, Madam, thank you. This is the lady I mentioned in my phone call," Kumar answered, gesturing towards me.

"And you are Mrs....?"

"I'm Mrs. Kiyama Fernando."

"And you're an English teacher?"

"Not exactly. I taught English literature in a few international schools in Colombo."

"But you're willing to teach general English here?"

"Yes..."

Mrs. Palpola looked thoughtful. "I must say this is very irregular. Teaching appointments are usually made by the Ministry of Education. We never hire teachers ourselves." She cleared her throat. "But then, this is a very unusual situation. If we wait until the Ministry sends a replacement, it will be next term. Priyanka was a good teacher, and he handled the higher grades. Those who are taking important exams this year. We can't afford to be without a teacher for months... If I contact the Ministry immediately, I can organize for a token salary to be paid utilizing our general funds. And you can start next week."

"How much would a token salary be?" I asked.

"I can't promise anything without consulting the relevant authorities," she hedged. *This woman would do well in politics!*

"Okay. Leaving that aside for the moment, I want to clarify a few things. Which grades will I be teaching exactly?"

"Grades six to eleven."

"Ah, so you don't have Advanced Level classes then?"

"No, not everyone opts to do their A' Levels. Those who qualify attend a school in Ratnapura town."

"And how many students are there in each class? How many classes per grade?"

"This is a small school, Mrs. Fernando. We have only about fifteen to twenty children per class and only one class per grade."

I liked the sound of that. "Can you tell me what the working hours will be like?"

"The school functions from 7:30 a.m. to 1:30 p.m."

"Yes, I know that, but since I will be on a token salary,

surely I needn't spend the entire day here. What is Priyanka's timetable like? I would prefer to just be present at those times instead," I explained.

Mrs. Palpola blinked. Obviously, such an arrangement had never occurred to her. Part time teachers must be unheard of here.

"I don't think we can allow that…"

"Look, Mrs. Palpola," I cut in tired of the red tape, "I'm here on holiday. I offered to fill in because Kumar and Vino here were talking about how the children will suffer because of this tragedy. As a teacher I felt obliged to offer my services. But I am not a government teacher. I never have been and never will be. I don't have the temperament, you see. I promise you, if I teach your students, I will cover the syllabus effectively and I will try to make the lessons as practical and interesting as I can. But I do have other things to do with my time and I'd rather not waste it hanging around here."

Mrs. Palpola fidgeted with her pen for a few seconds and then said, "Alright. I'll speak to the Ministry and get their permission. Can I have your contact details, to get back to you?"

Soon afterwards, we were back at the entrance to the building. I turned to Vino and Kumar and said, "Well, that went well!"

Kumar chuckled. "I don't think anyone has ever spoken to her like that! Teachers are highly respected in the community, and the principal is like a demi-god. People tend to bend over backwards to accommodate them. Their command is absolute in a school."

"I almost saw smoke shooting out of her ears when you told her you had better things to do with your time!" laughed Vino, as we reached our vehicle.

"I just hope she hires me. I got caught up in the moment and forgot that I need this job to solve our mystery," I said, shaking my head. "And thank you Kumar for setting this up. I hope you don't get blackballed because of me!"

"Oh, don't worry. She won't hold it against me. In fact, trying to help may have scored me some brownie points. Those come in handy when it's time for the election of prefects and so on, you know!"

With that he waved goodbye.

I checked my phone before driving off. "Oh, look, I've got a message from Trehan. He is inviting us for dinner today."

"Let's get back home soon and tell Manike she needn't cook then. I'm sure she'd love to be off early, if possible," said Vino as we drove off.

That evening I pulled out all my stylish clothes and wondered what to wear. It was not a date. It was not a party, either. A dinner invitation. I had not expected any fancy dinner outings during my stay, so my wardrobe was limited. In the end I decided on a batik dress. Unfortunately, I did not have all my accessories with me; I would have had to hire a moving van to bring everything!

Vino and I met in the hall. She was dressed in tight jeans that showed off her slim figure and a silk blouse. "Nice!" we said together as we surveyed each other.

"It's a good thing Manike has already left. I don't want her gossiping about us being dressed up and wondering where we're going," I commented.

We found our way to Trehan's mansion without too much difficulty; it was hard to miss. The massive white pillars and ornate cast iron gate we had seen on our cycle ride were imposing and impressive. Driving into the premises was like magically entering another land. The paddy fields and mud huts that were one hundred yards away seemed primitive in contrast. Extensive gardens surrounded the majestic three-story building which shone in the dark. A carved fountain topped by a marble swan in flight rose from the centre of the lawn. I noticed that the basin was dry: *the water pump must be under repairs*. I could see half-paved walkways winding off to either side of the building. On closer inspection, it was also clear that the gardens, though large, were not well-tended and the topiary needed pruning. *He needs to hire a good gardener!* The night was still, and surveying the odd mix of old and new, I wondered if anyone was at home. *Could the text have been a practical joke?*

The doorbell resounded with a clang, and as we waited, I whispered, "I wonder if there's a butler?" The door was opened by a maid (not in livery or uniform, as I had half expected), and we followed her into the hallway. Trehan emerged from an adjoining room immediately and showed us to some plush armchairs in the lobby.

"Thank you for joining me, ladies!" he said, expansively. "I've been wanting to show this place off before its grand opening. Please, take a seat while they bring some refreshments." He nodded to the maid. "So, what do you think so far?"

"The driveway probably looks better during the day," I said, "but this is amazing." The room was well lit, and the colourful furnishing and accessories were elegant. Obviously, no expense had been spared when redecorating the house. It truly looked like a small luxury hotel. A place where the rich and famous would come to unwind.

"I don't know what it looked like in your father's time, but if it was similar to the usual old ancestral homes in the area, well, you found one hell of an interior decorator!" Vino exclaimed.

When our drinks arrived Trehan stood and offered to show us around. He pointed out where the Reception Desk would be and took us through the many rooms on the ground floor. There was a Breakfast Room, a fine dining restaurant named Summer Fields, an impressive library, and various sitting rooms for guests to relax in.

"The first and second floors will house the guest rooms. On the third floor we have a gym and spa, and a rooftop area for private functions." He paused and looked at us expectantly, "Do you like it?"

"Like it? I love it!" I enthused. "You've got everything planned out. I can just picture visitors from all over the world enjoying themselves here. Were you in the hospitality industry when you were in the UK?"

Trehan laughed. "Oh, no. I'm a lawyer by profession, but I travel a lot and when I realized I inherited this place, I thought I'd shift gears and do something I've wanted to do for a while. It's nice to make a clean break and reroute your life, you know?"

"Yes," I murmured, "that I do."

"So," said Vino, "how soon can I make a booking at the spa?"

"Oh, there's a lot of work to be done yet. This place will be fully operational in about three months."

"Three months?" I moaned. "I won't be here in three months!"

"Ah, yes, I remember you said you were visiting. How long will you be staying?"

I nudged Vino and quipped, "As long as she can put up with me!"

I broke off as we stepped out at the back of the house. A thousand stars twinkled at us, at our feet. It took me a moment to realise we were gazing at a swimming pool. Vino gasped beside me. The effect was fantastic.

"And this is our pool. I had it newly installed, and we filled it with water only yesterday. I haven't even tried it out yet! The spa is not ready, but you are most welcome to swim a few laps anytime you wish."

It was definitely an attractive proposal. I was a competent swimmer, and I had used the pool regularly back in Colombo. Since I was not fond of the gaping, gasping crowds at the gyms, that was my only means of exercise. Of course, now that I was in the countryside, cycling up and down also helped.

We finished our pre-dinner drinks while surveying the pool and back gardens. There was as much space at the back of the building as there was in front. Since the hotel was on a rise the gardens descended in gradual tiers.

"This is a lovely place," I said, as we turned to go back in. "Did you grow up here?"

"Yes. I went to school in Ratnapura for a short while. Then moved on to study in Colombo. My father was a gem merchant, and we had an apartment in Colombo as well. So, it was term time there and vacations here, from when I was about eight."

"I'm sure your school friends would have loved visiting you out here!" commented Vino.

"Yes, and no," he answered. "There's a lot of room to run around, but no technology or modern entertainment. Lately, I've realized that that is ideal for the intuitive traveller who wants to escape the rat race and recharge his batteries… I'm sorry! I sound like a brochure!"

Vino and I laughed. I liked Trehan. He was charming and had a sense of humour.

Dinner was served in what was to become the Breakfast Room. Trehan explained that the Summer Fields restaurant was covered in unlaid tiles and electrical wiring. He also apologized for the meagre fare; his 5-star chef would be arriving in a few months. Until then, he made do with a cook from the village who was unaccustomed to western dishes.

"I'd kill for a good roast!" he joked, as we tucked into a meal of hoppers.

"These are quite good, you know," Vino remarked. "My cook, Manike, can't make hoppers. They look more like droopy, lumpy pancakes. These are nice and crispy!"

Over the rest of the meal we shared a bit of our lives. Vino talked about how she inherited and revamped the rubber plantation. I revealed the bare basics of my life and said I was on holiday. He glanced at my wedding band, but thankfully, did not pursue the subject.

"Who's running your gem business, now that you have branched out to this?" I asked, changing the subject.

"My mother. I'm an only child. But my heart's just not in that business, you know? We came to an agreement. She will let me try my hand at this. If it fails, I have to take over the gem business. If my hotel is a success, she will run things for now, and then set up a competent management to take over."

Trehan was a talker. As we listened to his plans and hopes for this new venture, I wondered how he managed to live in the middle of nowhere without an audience. *Maybe he speaks to a pet? No wonder he was desperate to make our acquaintance!*

"So, do you know anyone else in the area?" I asked, as we rose to leave.

"Not really. All my old classmates have vanished to God knows where. Most of Dad's gem industry friends are in Colombo, or overseas. That's why I'm breathing down the neck of my architect and contractor to get this place ready ASAP! Not that I'm complaining, I have a lot of work to do planning the launch and all that. But it would be nice to have people around once in a way…" He grinned at us and added, "Would you two be willing to drop in now and then? Like I said earlier, I wouldn't say no to some suggestions on how to improve!"

"I'm busy with the plantation most days, but I'm sure Kiyama would love to help out." said Vino. I frowned at her, but she just went on, "She's so bored, she volunteered to teach English for a pittance at the local school!"

Trehan looked at me in surprise. *Maybe I did not come across as the volunteering type?*

"That's a great gesture. But don't they have enough teachers?"

"Haven't you heard about the great mystery of the body in the paddy field?" asked Vino.

"Yes, I heard about that…"

"Well, Priyanka was the English teacher at the local school. And now they have no one to fill his post."

Trehan's eyes widened as he caught on. "So, you're helping out until they find a new teacher? That's a wonderful thing to do. Believe me, these kids need to learn the language if they are to move on. Why, just the other day I was wondering how I am going to find staff who can converse in English!" He broke off and said sheepishly, "Oh dear, there I go again. Please, excuse me. I keep coming back to my work…"

"It's okay," I said, "it shows that you are passionate about what you are doing."

It was late when we bid him goodbye. *Time does fly when you are enjoying yourself.*

Vino would not stop talking, as we drove back. She seemed to have caught Trehan's verbal diarrhoea. "I like him. And I think he's quite taken with you. I saw him checking out your wedding band – you really need to take that thing off, it's giving mixed signals. You don't want to come across as married, but available!"

"It's separated, but available then, is it?" I asked, amused. "When did you get so familiar with modern dating terminology?"

"Social media, darling! You need to be active online to know the latest. Anyway, here's the plan. Let's try out his pool as soon as possible. I'm sure he would look hot in trunks!"

I blushed. This conversation was taking a path I would much rather avoid.

"What about our investigation? Aren't you worried about the police anymore?"

"That seems to have hit a snag, hasn't it? I mean what more can we do right now? We need to get you into the school, but we have to wait for Mrs. Palpola to call. So, let's enjoy life a little. Come on, Kiyama, let your hair down!"

"I have short hair," I reminded her, as I drove.

The next few days were quiet, as Vino predicted. Our investigation had hit a wall. I mooched around the house during the day and took long rides exploring the countryside in the evenings. On Friday, the much-anticipated call from Mrs. Palpola came through – I was to start work next week. Over the weekend I joined Vino on a shopping expedition to Eheliya to stock up on essentials that are unavailable in town and visited Trehan for Sunday lunch and a dip in the pool.

Little did I know that it was the quiet before the storm.

CHAPTER EIGHT

PLEATS. MY FINGERS ached with all that pleating. Yards and yards of pleats…

This is why I hate sarees. Someone who has never worn one may wonder where all the cloth goes. Well, much of it goes into the pleats. You need to keep your fingers steady so that the size of the pleats does not vary. In one way, I was lucky. Since Vino favoured cotton sarees I did not have to contend with the cloth cascading through my fingers. We needed some large pins to keep the pleats in place, though. Who would have guessed that grown women would depend on nappy pins to keep their clothes up? But, yes, those are what we used. Any other safety pin would just bend and break. But industrial strength nappy pins do the job perfectly. I would have never survived the battle if not for Vino. Although she claimed to never wear sarees herself, she was a lot more proficient than I was. I would have given up in tears if not for her intervention.

After waging war with my attire for about half an hour I finally surveyed myself in the mirror. Oh, and that is another essential requirement when getting into this outfit – a full length mirror. Otherwise, your saree would be too long, and that is a recipe for disaster. *Lipstick, or no lipstick?* I selected a light pink and touched it to my lips. I forewent the rest of my makeup since I did not want streaks running down my face in the heat. The person who looked back at me did not look like a government schoolteacher. My short hair, brown eyes, shaped eyebrows, and fair skin screamed 'I am from Colombo!' I sighed. Well, at least I was making an effort to blend in by wearing this contraption and if they did not like what they saw, it was their loss!

"Well, I'm as ready as I'll ever be," I announced.

"Just remember to hold the front pleats up when walking up stairs," cautioned Vino. "And fold the pota around you when you sit down."

"Maybe I should just stand still and not walk or sit?" I

asked, with a grin.

She grinned back and said, "You'll do fine. You're a fantastic teacher. Those kids won't know what hit them!"

Reassured by that and armed with my handbag and some stationary, I made my way to my car. And, hit my first obstacle. I have never driven a car in a saree! It took me three tries to sit comfortably without getting twisted into a pretzel.

"Oh, and Kiy," said Vino through the window, "remember to take your pota into the car with you before you shut the door!"

I made my way to the principal's office as soon as I entered the building. The air was abuzz with the sounds of children talking and laughing.

"Ah! Mrs. Fernando!" said Mrs. Palpola when she saw me. "You're early. Please take a seat until I find someone to show you around." She handed me a piece of paper. "This is the timetable. Like I said, you're teaching grades six to eleven. They each have English twice a week. And you can come in late and leave early, as you requested."

The door opened and a student poked her head in. "You

wanted to see a prefect, Madam?"

"Yes, Thushari. This is our new English teacher, Kiyama Madam. Please take her to the staff room and show her Priyanka Sir's shelf, and then take her around the school and show her the classes from grade six to eleven. She needs to be in grade ten by the third period."

I stood. "Thank you, Mrs. Palpola."

Thushari was shy and quiet. She did not speak to me as we walked down the corridor but stared studiously at the floor while we walked. So, I decided to pepper her with questions.

"Which grade are you in, Thushari?"

"Grade eleven, Madam."

"Oh, please call me Miss Kiyama. I'm not old enough to be a Madam."

She giggled. "Yes, Miss."

"Shouldn't you be in class?"

"This is our PT period, Miss."

"I didn't see any students outside the school when I drove in. Is there a playground at the back?"

"Yes, Miss."

This girl was so reticent, it was like pulling teeth! I decided to try one more time.

"So, Thushari, do you like English?"

"Oh, yes, Miss! It's a refreshing change to the other harder subjects like science and maths."

"Was Priyanka Sir a good teacher?"

She looked down and twisted her hands. "He was Miss. He got us to actually do the dialogues and so on in the class, unlike the teacher before him."

I smiled and said, "Then I have a lot to live up to!"

By then, we had reached the staff room. It was empty. She led me in and gestured towards a cupboard filled with books. "Priyanka Sir used the second shelf."

She waited outside while I rummaged through the books. All the government textbooks were there, along with a stack of exercise books belonging to students of grade eight. I consulted my timetable and chose the ones I would need for the day.

Next, Thushari dutifully showed me each classroom. The lower grades were on the ground floor and the O' Level classes were on the first floor, with the small library, computer room, and laboratory. I thought they were quite well-equipped, for a small school.

"Are you doing your O' Levels in December, Thushari?" I asked, to make conversation as we walked.

"Yes, Miss."

"So, you will be leaving this school and attending another in Ratnapura?"

"Yes, Miss."

"Which stream of study are you hoping to do for your A' Levels?"

"I want to be a doctor so I'm hoping to do science."

We stopped. We had reached our final destination. "Well, all the best, Thushari!" I wished her as she left me at the door to Grade 10.

The bell rang. I could see an elderly teacher finishing up inside. The blackboard was covered in mathematical equations. She smiled at me as we crossed paths. "Are you the new English teacher?"

"Yes, I'm Kiyama."

"I'm Manori. Good luck on your first day! I'll see you in the staffroom during break."

The room was crowded with desks set in rows. The walls were colourful and proudly displayed charts pertaining to many subjects. The class comprising both boys and girls since this was a co-ed school stood up to greet me as I entered.

"Good Morning, Madam!"

"Good Morning! But, please, call me Miss Kiyama." I sighed inwardly. *This was going to be my refrain for the rest of the week.* "As you probably know, I'm taking over your English lessons. Can someone tell me which lesson was covered last with Priyanka Sir?"

No answer. They all just looked at me.

"Oh no. Are they too shy, or can't they understand the basics?" I tried again. "I'm not going to bite you!" I said, jovially. "Which lesson did you do last?"

Finally, one boy said, "Lesson fourteen, Miss."

Feeling relieved, I said, "Then turn to that page, and let's do that one again."

Half an hour later, they were a lot friendlier and more relaxed as we waited for the bell to go. I decided to spend the last few minutes getting to know them and the school. We played a name game that left them howling with laughter.

"Thank you, Miss! That lesson was fun!" said one boy, whose name, I had just learned, was Kasun. "You're a much better teacher than Priyanka Sir!"

Half the class shushed him, while the others looked on in

interest.

"Oh, and why do you say that? I heard that he was giving extra tuition and using new games in his classes."

"My father said he's a corrupt individual and his teaching skills are of no use with a personality like that!"

Some of his classmates objected loudly.

"Do you know why your father said that?" I inquired, with my fingers crossed. It was a long shot that a teenager would know the gory details, but I needed to ask.

"Erm… nothing…" he muttered as he backed down.

Not wanting to make a scene in front of twenty other children, I made a mental note to find a quiet moment to pursue the matter with him later.

This pattern of extreme reticence which I had to break down like attacking an enemy fortress followed me through the day. It was exhausting. I wished for the more vociferous and carefree youngsters I was accustomed to in Colombo. *What is it that makes children from small towns so shy? Is it the education system they are used to? Do the other teachers browbeat them into silence?* I pondered this as I made my way back to the staff room during the interval.

This time the room was full of male and female teachers. I

stepped in and looked for a free space to sit down.

"Miss Kiyama!" called a voice from my right. It was the mathematics teacher, Miss Manori. "Please join us here!"

She was seated with two other ladies. They were having their midday snack. I took out the sandwich Manike had wrapped and sat down. Manori introduced me to the other two teachers who taught civics and science. After giving them a highly censored background to my life and career, I listened quietly as they resumed their previous conversation.

"Have you covered the syllabus?" asked Manori.

The civics teacher, Yalani, nodded. "I'm doing some revision now."

The science teacher, Chandrika, added, "You're lucky the civics syllabus isn't too long!"

They all laughed.

Manori turned to me. "So, Kiyama, how has your day been so far?"

"I can't complain," I answered, not wanting to sound negative at the outset. "Priyanka had covered most of the syllabus, so I don't have much to do. The kids are nice but getting them to speak is such a challenge!"

"Hmm..." said Yalani, "I suppose speaking out is an

important part of a language lesson. Honestly, though, it's easier to cover the syllabus when there are no interruptions."

I bit my tongue and decided not to comment on that. Instead, I asked, "I heard that Priyanka was almost appointed as Sectional Head. I guess it's lucky he didn't get the job. Finding a replacement for that would not be as easy as finding someone to teach his subject."

Manori nodded. "To be honest, we all expected him to get that post. But the Principal recommended Mr. Bandara and he's now the Sectional Head for grades nine to eleven."

"What does Mr. Bandara teach?"

"He's the Sinhala language teacher. He's seated over there." Manori tilted her chin towards a tall, thin, bespectacled male teacher in the corner.

I leaned in. "Don't tell anyone this, but I also heard that Priyanka had complained about the injustice of that. A girl in town told us Priyanka claimed Bandara had bribed the Principal!"

They exchanged shocked glances.

"You seem to know more about what is happening than we do!" Manori said, finally. Then, changing the subject, she asked, "We heard you are here on holiday. How has it been so far?"

"Oh, so so," I replied. "It's been a lot more exciting than anticipated, what with the body in the paddy field. My friend Vino told me about Priyanka. She's the new owner of The Orchard Rubber Plantation."

"Tall, slim, long hair?" asked Yalani. "Did she know Priyanka? It's just that I was in town on Saturday afternoon and I saw them having a cup of tea outside the bakery."

"Yes, she knew him a little, I think." I paused. "Why do you ask?"

"Well… they were in a heated argument that day. I was on the opposite side of the road, but I heard their raised voices. Priyanka slammed his cup down and walked off in a huff." She looked at me expectantly.

My heart beat faster and I drew in a sharp breath. *Vino had lied to the police when they asked about the argument!* I would have to ask her about it when I got home.

"At least he was alive when he left," I commented. "That's something."

Yalani dropped her voice and leaned forward. "I heard that he had been poisoned. It may not have had an effect until later!"

Manori looked alarmed. "Now, now, Yalani! Let's not speculate. Vino is Kiyama's friend. I'm sure she did nothing wrong!"

Ignoring the rising doubt inside me I nodded emphatically and agreed. "And anyway, it would take some clever sleight of hand to put insecticide into a cup of tea in a cramped bakery! And I doubt it would taste good at all! Did you see where he went next?"

"Once I finished my shopping and came out again, I saw him in the distance walking past the paddy fields on the Eheliya road. Your friend was nowhere to be seen."

Just then, the bell rang, tolling an end to our discussion. Overall, it had been a fruitful half an hour, and had given me much to think about. I had just jumped to her defence but inside I still had my doubts. *Why had Vino lied to the police? Was it just nerves? Or did she have something to hide?* My heart said to trust her, but my mind asked, '*Did I really know her?*'

The rest of the morning was uneventful, and I was able to leave by noon. I did not gather any other interesting titbits of news, and no one else had anything to say about Priyanka, Mr. Bandara or the Principal. The children mostly agreed that he was a good teacher and would be missed. I kept an eye out for Kasun from my first class who had voiced a dislike for the teacher. But I did not see him that day. Finding out why he had such a strong negative view and what he knew would be at the top of my list of things to do tomorrow.

I was unable to have a heart-to-heart with Vino that afternoon. When I returned from the school she met me at the door, waving a note.

"Do you remember the farmer's daughter, Sumu?"

"Yes..." I replied, as I walked in and collapsed into an armchair.

"She wants to see us in the evening!"

I perked up. We had asked her to share any news with us. *Maybe she had discovered who last saw Priyanka!*

After jumping out of my saree and into more comfortable clothes and having a hasty lunch we were cycling our way back to the paddy field. I watched Vino as we rode. Her eyes were shining with excitement and she set a frantic pace. *Would she be so eager to meet Sumu if she had poisoned him at the bakery? Maybe she was looking for someone who had met him later that evening so that she could pass the blame on to them? How long did it take for insecticide to work anyway?*

As we locked our bikes in the usual place, Vino asked me why I was so quiet. I told her I was recovering from my first day at school. We made our way to the small huts lining the field. Sumu's younger brother was playing with some other boys. He stuck his head into his house and shouted, "Akka!!!" when he saw us.

Vino grabbed my arm and said, "Remember to play your part!"

"My part?" I asked, momentarily confused. And then it dawned on me. Of course! I had pretended to be a ditzy city-dweller the last time I was here. I looked around and commented in a loud voice, "Where are those adorable chickens we saw the last time we were here?"

Sumu's brother made a show of smacking his lips and said, "They were quite tasty!"

I looked at him blankly. Then, opened my eyes wide in horror and exclaimed, "You *ate* them?"

The boy mimed wringing a neck. He seemed to be enjoying himself. It is not every day that you get to terrorize visitors from Colombo.

I was having fun. Giving it all I had I threw my hands up and wailed, "Oh! The poor little chickens! And I was so looking forward to feeding them some corn today!"

By then, Sumu had arrived. She shook her head and escorted us away from the boys who were sniggering at my performance.

Vino took over. "We got your message. What did you find out?"

Sumu looked around as if checking to see that no one could hear us. "I spoke to some of the workers in this area. Quite a few people remember seeing Priyanka Sir walking out of town that Saturday evening. The thing is…" she paused. "The thing is he always rode his bicycle when he visited me, rather than walk from the school lodgings. But he was on foot that day, it seems. I thought that was weird."

I looked at them and asked, "Maybe he decided to walk for exercise rather than ride?"

They both shook their heads and Vino answered my question. "Priyanka didn't like to walk. He had one of those new-fangled bikes with gears. You don't have to make any real effort to pedal. And a bike gets you to your destination faster. He was always rushing from one place to another."

"Yes," Sumu agreed. "He seemed to have a packed schedule all the time." She shrugged. "I always wondered whether it was just for show…"

I mulled on this. "So, why would he then choose to walk?"

"Maybe his bike needed repairs?" offered Sumu.

"Or, he could have been meeting someone in a car?" ventured Vino.

"Anyone who had enough money to pay him to keep quiet would also own a car," I agreed. "If someone gave him a lift, they could have driven anywhere from there!"

Sumu gasped, "Pay him? To keep quiet? As in *blackmail?*"

I wanted to kick myself. I should not have mentioned that in front of her, but the damage was done so I covered up the best I could. "It's just a guess. We suspect he may have known something. Something that got him killed. But, please, don't talk about it. We don't want to spread unsubstantiated stories! For one thing, the police would not be happy…"

At the mention of the police, she nodded.

"I remember seeing a sign in the shop where I purchased my bike, that they also undertake repairs," I went on. "Since it's just at the other end of town why don't we check that out immediately and find out whether his bike had any problems that day?"

"Thank you, Sumu, you've been a big help," Vino said, as she handed her some cash. Sumu shook her head but Vino insisted. "Please, your information means a lot. Buy yourself something nice and celebrate life!"

Sumu accepted the cash shyly.

Vino and I discussed possibilities as we made our way back to the main road.

"Did you find out anything interesting at the school?" she

asked.

"There was one boy who seemed to dislike him. He quoted his father as saying 'He's a corrupt individual'. I want to find out who he is and whether Priyanka knew his family."

"Hey, that's a great lead. Maybe Priyanka found out something about the boy's father and he in turn shared his frustration with his son!"

I watched her carefully as we mounted our bikes. "So far we seem to have very few suspects."

"Oh, I wouldn't say that," she called back. "There's the farmer."

"What? Sumu's father? I thought we ruled him out?"

"We can't just rule someone out. Sumu's a nice girl and loyal to her family. But she did reveal that her father was mad at Priyanka."

"But she broke off their relationship some time ago. And she's not pregnant or anything, and no one is accusing him of rape, so her father wouldn't have a motive," I pointed out.

"Okay. There's the parent from the school."

"We need to find out more about that one."

"And the money lender."

"He's definitely a creep, but we didn't find out anything that points to him killing Priyanka. And, he said he didn't deal in blackmail."

"If you believe him, that is. I mean, the guy's a criminal. Can we believe anything he says?" she asked.

"Good point," I conceded.

My mind was still in turmoil as we turned into Main Street. And then another thought jumped in. "Vino, you met Priyanka that Saturday. Didn't you notice that he was not on his bicycle?"

Vino frowned, pedalling hard. "Not really. He was already at the bakery when I got there… I didn't look for a bike… And after out chat I was a little upset and I didn't watch him leave…"

We stopped by the bicycle repair shop. "We need to look into motive and means for each of the suspects," I said. "Let's make a list when we get home."

The trip to the repair shop turned out to be a waste of time. Priyanka had never handed his bike in. According to the proprietor, the machine was brand new.

"Where is it, then?" wondered Vino, as we set off for home.

"The bike? Possibly at the teacher's lodgings. I'll see if I can find out tomorrow."

CHAPTER NINE

VINO AND I sat outside in the veranda after dinner.

I drew a table in my exercise book listing the suspects, means, and motive.

"Right," I said, when I was ready, "let's start with the farmer. What was his name? Laksiri?"

"Yes. He had the means. I'm sure there are many bottles of insecticide lying around there."

"But how would he get Priyanka to drink it? I mean, he had just made a fool of the farmer's daughter. I don't see them seated by the paddy field sharing a cup of tea!"

Vino laughed. "You're right. It is unlikely. Let's move on. What about Ariyawansa?"

I considered it. "We know that Priyanka liked to gamble. He had racked up some debt. Ariyawansa didn't correct us when we asked about Priyanka's debts. So, he must have initially borrowed to keep his gambling addiction going. That's a clever scam, by the way. People come to you to gamble and then borrow from you to pay their debts!"

"Means and motive," muttered Vino, looking out into the dark garden. "Priyanka would have sat down for a strong drink with Ariyawansa, if he was invited to do so. And I'm sure the criminal underworld has easy access to substances a lot worse than insecticide! But, Ariyawansa has no motive, does he?"

I sighed. "No, he doesn't. He got his money back. Even if he were blackmailing Priyanka in turn, killing him would equal slaughtering the goose that laid the golden eggs. It doesn't add up."

I looked at my paper. "That leaves… the parent, the Sinhala teacher Mr. Bandara, and the Principal of the school Mrs. Palpola. I asked as discreetly as I could about the possibility of bribery. The teachers I spoke to admitted they were taken aback by Bandara's appointment but if it did happen as we suspect, no one is willing to talk about it or make an accusation outright. Mr. Bandara lives at the school lodgings, same as Priyanka. I can't go in there since I'm a part timer, and anyway, it's men only. I asked around in-between classes. The lady teachers are all from the vicinity. The Principal lives on the outskirts of town but not in the direction Priyanka was walking in. So, he couldn't have been going to see her."

"Means and motive," Vino repeated. "Bandara had the means. They could have had a drink before Priyanka left on his errand. I can't see how Mrs. Palpola could have poisoned him, though. It was a Saturday. She and Priyanka would not have been at the school. And I doubt she would have appreciated a male teacher visiting her at her residence out of the blue."

"So, I'll have to find out more about Bandara's movements, and the parent, tomorrow." I glanced at her as something occurred to me. "What about Kumar?"

She looked at me blankly. "What about him?"

"Could he be involved?"

Vino laughed at the idea, but I continued doggedly. "He knew Priyanka from way back. People get up to all sorts of weird and illegal activities when they're in university. Maybe there was something Priyanka knew about Kumar."

"The thought didn't even cross my mind," Vino admitted.

"Either you are very good at this, or you have an overactive imagination!"

I smiled grimly, then paused to take a fortifying breath. *It's now or nothing... but I have to know...* "And... there's you..."

Vino froze. "Me? Are you saying *I'm* a suspect? I thought we started this to prove otherwise!"

"Hang on!" I said, as she got up to leave. "Please, hear me out. I have a few questions, that's all. There are some things I don't understand... Please, Vino..."

I waited for her to resume her seat and then ploughed on. "Inspector de Silva mentioned text messages. Did Priyanka ask you to meet him that day?"

Vino would not meet my eyes. She looked away and muttered, "Yes."

"Can I know what it was about? People on the street heard you two arguing. The police would have heard that story by now, so there's no point denying it if they ask you again."

And then it hit me. *They had not been in a romantic relationship as she first claimed.* "Was he blackmailing *you*?"

My heart almost broke as Vino broke down in tears. "Yes," she whispered. "He found out about me."

What illegal activity could she have possibly been a part of to attract a blackmailer?

"That I'm a lesbian."

There was an awkward pause. I was unsure what to say. Although I had suspected it for years, this was not a subject we had ever openly discussed. "How did he find out? I mean, I know some people are very open about their way of life, but you're a private person. You don't flaunt it or throw it in people's faces."

"I'm sorry, Kiy. I should have told you all of this right at the beginning," she sniffed, "but you and everyone else jumped to the conclusion that he and I had had an affair, and that was too good an opportunity to pass. I thought, if no one knows about the blackmail, then there's no harm done. I thought, if I lie and pretend we had been close, then no one would dig deeper." She paused. "I should have known that the police would read his messages. I should have confided in you."

"Yes," I said, "you should have. But there's nothing we can do about that now. And there's nothing to be ashamed of. Can you at least confide in me now?"

Vino squared her shoulders. "Like I said, he figured out my secret. My family know, and my crowd in Colombo. But out here? I've been wary about how I behave. I'm a newcomer, trying to run a business. Being a woman is bad enough in this misogynistic society. You wouldn't believe the backlash I had to face when my male cousins realized that my uncle had left the plantation to me. Only the knowledge of my sexual preferences prevented them from accusing me of sleeping with my own uncle! I mean, that's really twisted! It's sick!

"I was suffering through all that when I moved here last year. At that welcoming party, Priyanka did hit on me. I just brushed it off as innocent flirting. But he just wouldn't give up! In the end, I told him I wasn't interested. I think he put two and two together. It was probably a lucky guess. He couldn't have had any evidence as such. But people will always believe the worst and say no smoke without fire, you know? So, I paid what he asked for. In hindsight, that was a stupid thing to do because it confirmed his suspicions. And, once I was in the mess there was no getting out...I kept thinking, what if the people in town and those I work with find out. I wouldn't be able to get anything done or work with anyone. They'd shun me. I'm not naïve. I know what small towns are like..."

This was worse than I had expected. "Does Kumar know?"

She laughed harshly. "Kumar? Ha! He'd run a mile! You saw how strait-laced he is. He's my right-hand man. I can't afford to lose him. The entire plantation would shut down if people gave in their notice just because they didn't approve of my sexuality!"

"What are you saying, Vino? Did you kill him?" I did not want to ask, but I had to know.

To my intense relief, she shook her head vehemently. "No, I didn't. I may have done something in a few months, but I hadn't reached breaking point. Obviously, he pushed someone else too far, and they got their revenge first."

"But you seemed genuinely upset at his death!"

"I was. It was all so sudden. I had wished for it so hard, and then one day – Bam! If I were a religious fundamentalist, I'd say it was the hand of God. I didn't know what to think. What to feel. I was relieved. I was upset at the violence of it all. I felt guilty for rejoicing at his death…"

I reflected on that for a moment and nodded. *If this were a tall story, it would definitely take the cake.* It was unexpected enough to be the truth. Whoever said truth is stranger than fiction sure knew what they were talking about!

Then, I suddenly realized something. "The police! Once they read Priyanka's messages, they'll know it was not a romantic relationship. Did he ever text you a request for money? Anything which would incriminate him?"

Vino stared out at the garden thoughtfully. "Not that I recall… It was always rather vague… a request to meet me somewhere… or something like, 'I was able to pay the bills today' to indicate that the money had been transferred to his account..."

"But the police might figure it out! And blackmail is a lot worse than a botched romance. You have to tell them the truth rather than hide it if they ask again: lies will only make you look more suspicious. And you must insist that you didn't have the opportunity to kill him."

Vino squirmed and did not agree to my proposal. Well, it was her life and her call. However, I could always set the record straight if they came ready to clap her in handcuffs. She may not thank me for it now, but I was ready to do anything to keep her out of jail.

"We need to be ready for when the police come around. Why did he ask you to meet him that evening?"

She studied her fingers for a moment and then said softly, "He wanted more money."

"And you said...?"

"I said no! I run a rubber plantation, not a gold mine! I told him I'd tell the cops and hang my reputation!"

"And that was it?"

"Yes, he made some nasty sexist remarks and stormed off." She peered up at me. "I couldn't have killed him even if I had wanted to, you know. There were witnesses!"

"What about later in the evening? Do you have an alibi in case the police suggest you met him afterwards? What did you do when you returned from the bakery?"

"I came back here, had a good cry, and turned the music on loud."

"And Saturday is Manike's day off, so there's no one to back up your story." I was beginning to feel quite defeated. I liked reading mystery novels but being in one was not as fun as I expected. "Did you get a phone call, reply to an email, anything?" Then, I stopped. "*That's it*! That's the night *I* called you! Maybe there is a God looking after us because something put it in my mind to give you a ring!" I was so exhilarated I wanted to run a lap around the garden.

Vino grasped my hands. "Andy's shenanigans prompted you to call me. I should send him a Thank You card!"

"He wasn't good for nothing after all!"

That sent us into fits of laughter. I even hugged her and did a little dance. Our neighbours must have wondered if we had hit the liquor cabinet.

"I'm so sorry. I was so caught up in the drama of my own life, I was completely blind to what you were going through. I didn't even notice that you were upset when I called that night! Either you're one heck of an actress, or I'm a selfish bitch. I thought having a cheating husband was bad, but this? This is right out of a suspense novel!"

"Let's celebrate!" she said, the relief evident as she headed for the kitchen. "I think we deserve some cheese, wine, and chocolate!"

The police visited our house a lot sooner than expected. They were at the front door sharp and early the next morning. I was about to wrestle with my saree when the unwelcome figure of Inspector de Silva rang the bell. Manike had also just arrived, so we had an avid audience for this encounter.

"Miss Dias, we'd like you to come with us to the police station. We have a few more questions regarding your relationship with Priyanka Sir."

The dreaded words – 'come with us to the police station'! Vino and I both paled. I was in a bind. I wanted to go with her, but I could not take leave on my second day at work.

Inspector de Silva must have read my face, because he said, "You can't come with her, Mrs. Fernando, unless you are her lawyer."

Lawyer! That was it!

"I'll call Trehan. He said he's a lawyer by profession, remember? He may be able to advise you," I told Vino as I ran to my bedroom.

Everything happened so fast. I made the call and Trehan promised to meet them at the police station at Eheliya. He also promised to keep me appraised of events via text messages since I would not be able to answer the phone while teaching. I dressed as best as I could on my own. Two sore thumbs and half an hour later I was ready. I knew Vino was innocent; our conversation yesterday had proved that. But we still did not know who the guilty party was. Handing that information to the police was our best bet, so I had more than one job to do at the school today. Keeping that firmly in mind I left for work.

Vino had already left with the police officers by the time I stepped back into the hall. Manike was hovering by the kitchen doorway, a look of shocked incomprehension on her face.

"Has she been arrested?" she asked.

"No," I said firmly. "She's only helping them to catch the real murderer."

The drive to the school helped to clear my mind. I had three tasks today. First, to find more information about the parent who may have been blackmailed. Second, to locate Priyanka's missing bicycle. Third, to check on Bandara's movements that weekend. The answer to my second task appeared as I parked my vehicle. There was a security guard on duty today who helped me manoeuvre into the correct spot. I had not seen him around previously. Taking Rs 500 out of my wallet, I got down.

"Good morning," I greeted him.

"Morning, Miss."

"I didn't see you yesterday. I sure could have used the help to park!"

He smiled. "I wasn't feeling too well yesterday, Miss. Are you a new teacher?"

I answered in the affirmative and added, "I'm filling Priyanka Sir's post for a few days until the Ministry sends a permanent teacher."

He nodded sagely. "Those pencil pushers at the Ministry take forever to do anything. We don't even get paid on time, some months."

That was my cue. "Listen," I said, "Can you do me a small favour? You know the bicycle Priyanka used to ride? It's gone missing. A friend of mine bet that I can't figure out what happened to it. Do you think you could keep an eye out for it and let me know if you find it?"

I handed him the money. "Here, keep this for your trouble."

I knew it was a lame excuse, but it was the best I could come up with on the spur of the moment. He hesitated, so I chatted on. "I suppose someone would have to find the bike sooner or later. I mean, his family would want his belongings sent back to them, right?"

He considered that and finally accepted the note. "Sure thing, Miss."

Feeling relieved that at least one part of this mystery would be solved by the end of the day, I turned and entered the building. I was fairly familiar with the layout by now and made my way to my first lesson without getting lost. My mind was not on my work. I rushed through the lessons, setting the students as many writing tasks as I could so that I could check my phone for messages from Trehan.

Finally, as I was walking to the staffroom during the interval, my phone pinged. I stopped dead in my tracks and dug it out of my bag.

Vino explained everything to their satisfaction. She's back home now.

Can we meet for dinner to celebrate?

I texted back:

Will speak to Vino and confirm dinner.

Thank you for being there for her – you're a life saver!

Feeling much better I entered the staffroom and looked for Miss Manori and her gang. They were in the same seats as yesterday. I pulled up a chair and joined them.

"I hope you don't mind my eating with you?"

"Of course, not," said Manori, making room for me at the table.

I surveyed the room, looking for Bandara.

He was speaking to a colleague at the other end. Luckily, they were near the cupboard that held my textbooks. I smiled and commented on the conversation around my table for a few minutes as I formulated a course of action. When I was ready, I excused myself and walked over to the cupboard. I opened it and leaned in as if searching for something. As I had hoped, I was able to eavesdrop on the conversation nearby.

Bandara was talking about a training workshop he had recently attended and explaining some of the proposed changes to the syllabus which would come into effect next year. His friend spent some time complaining about bureaucrats and their inane need to keep fixing things that didn't need to be fixed, and then said, "At least you got a short holiday out of it, no?"

Bandara replied, "Yes, it was good to leave the town for a few days. I know our lodgings are better than most, but we are nearing the end of the term and I was longing for a break!"

"You missed all the excitement, though," commented the other teacher.

Bandara made an indelicate noise. "I don't want to have anything to do with Priyanka, alive or dead, thank you very much!"

I froze in my bogus search for books. *What was that? It sounded as if Bandara had been away on his workshop last weekend...* I grabbed the books I needed, stood up and muttered, "Ow, my back!" and returned to my seat. I paid little attention to the heated discussion around me. Apparently, the new board of prefects was to be chosen before the end of the school year and there was stiff competition.

My thoughts were on our murder mystery. Since Bandara was out of town last weekend, we could cross him off our list. That left only the parent. *Now, how was I going to ask a kid about his father's misdoings?*

Fate intervened yet again. I caught the name 'Kasun

Dissanayake' in the discussion around me, and I focused on what they were saying.

Chandrika was talking. "I like that boy. He's studious and competent. And he comes from a good family."

Personally, I could not see what a child's family had to do with prefectship, but I asked, "What do his parents do?"

"His mother is a housewife, of course, but his father is the manager of the local Commercial Bank. I think Kasun will follow in his father's footsteps. He has a keen mind."

"That's useful to know. I need to open an account and I can ask for him by name," I said brightly, as I filed the information away.

I had all the answers I needed! I am usually a diligent and conscientious teacher, but I spent the rest of the day checking my phone for the time. I had so many things to do outside. If patience is a virtue I was overflowing with vice. I made the barest effort in the classes and rushed out as soon as I was done for the day. I was thrilled to see the security guard seated by the gate. I was the only one leaving at the time, so I slowed down to talk to him as I was driving out.

"Were you able to find the bike?" I asked.

"Yes, Miss," he said, with a grin. "That task was dead easy. Priyanka Sir's bike is leaning against the wall of the teachers' lodgings. I don't think it will be there for much longer though. Some drug addict is sure to steal it."

"Then it's a good thing we looked now. Thank you so much!" I said, and before he could ask me any awkward questions, I put the car in gear and sped off.

Vino was resting in the hall when I reached home. Obviously, the events of the day had been stressful, and she had decided to take another day's leave. I joined her as soon as I had untangled myself from my saree.

"Well," I said, "what happened? Trehan sent me a very brief text. I want all the details!"

She sank back into the cushions of the sofa. "You were right, Kiy. They had gone through the messages and concluded that I was hiding something. I really should thank you for questioning me last night. It was so much easier to explain things. I told them about Priyanka trying to blackmail me without divulging why. I said it's too personal and they let it go. I also said I couldn't have possibly poisoned his tea and you are my alibi for later in the evening, so they may want to talk to you next to verify matters, though."

I shrugged. "I'll tell them the truth. No sweat. Or they may just check your phone records. How was Trehan by the way?"

Vino giggled. "He's a corporate lawyer! We never asked what his specialization was. He just sat with me and looked serious, but I think having a lawyer there helped keep them in check."

"Oh, before I forget," I said, "Trehan invited us over to dinner today. We'll have to share our findings with him after dragging him in like that."

"I think he's earned it! And, who knows, he may be able to shine some light on the puzzle."

"Which reminds me, I got a whole lot of answers at the school today. Priyanka's bicycle is at the lodgings, so he chose to walk that evening. Bandara was out of town last weekend so he couldn't have done it, and Kasun's father is the manager of the Commercial Bank in town. I know it's a long shot, and we have nothing to indicate he was blackmailed, but it's the only lead we've got left."

Vino looked at me quizzically. "Do we need to pursue this now? I mean, I'm obviously off the hook and I've proved to the police that I have a good alibi. Maybe we should just leave it to them to catch the killer."

I made a face. I was too involved in the case now. I didn't want to give up, and I told her so. "If you've had enough, I'll visit the bank this afternoon, just to satisfy my curiosity. You needn't come."

"Of course I'll come with you!" she said. "You've done so much for me. It's all I can do to help you."

We confirmed our dinner date with Trehan and rode into town after lunch.

I had not lied when I said I needed to open an account. If I was going to spend some time here, I would need access to cash. We walked in just before closing time and asked to speak to the manager, Mr. Dissanayake. The clerk was not happy but showed us in. As always, well-tailored clothes and a refined manner opened many doors.

Mr. Dissanayake was a short, thin man in thick-rimmed spectacles. He looked up from his computer screen, smiled and shook hands with us as we walked in.

"Good afternoon, Miss…?"

"I'm Mrs. Kiyama Fernando," I answered with a smile. "I'm going to be in the area for a while and I want to open an account with your bank so that I can transfer some money in from Colombo."

"Of course, that's a very simple matter," he said. I got the impression he was wondering why I had bothered him for such a trivial request, so I continued with, "You see. I have premier accounts in Colombo and there was such a long queue outside..."

I could see Vino trying to conceal a grin. The ploy worked, though. Mr. Dissanayake immediately sat up and nodded. "That's understandable. We will get the necessary forms and have everything ready in no time."

While we waited for the forms to arrive, I smiled and said, "Actually, Mr. Dissanayake, I asked for you because I've heard such wonderful things about your son. You see, I'm volunteering at the school, filling in Priyanka Sir's post until they find a permanent replacement. Your son, Kasun, is in one of my classes."

His face lost its affable smile as soon as I mentioned Priyanka's name. I exchanged a glance with Vino, and she nodded. She had noticed it too. He started to play with the pen on his table. I decided to delve further.

"Of course, it's not easy to fill his shoes. From everything I hear, Priyanka was a very capable teacher. Everyone seems to have loved him."

I hoped I was not laying it on too thick, but he fell for the bait.

"I don't know who you have been talking to, but Priyanka was only human. He had his faults." By now, Mr. Dissanayake was gripping his pen in both hands.

"We did hear some ugly rumours about gambling and blackmail, but I'm sure those were created by his rivals trying to tarnish his memory…" I offered, tentatively.

"Don't take this wrong, Mrs. Fernando, but sometimes, there is no smoke without fire!"

I feigned surprise. "Oh! I didn't realise you knew him."

"Yes," he almost growled. "I knew him. He and I were in school together for a few years when we were younger. It's incredible how some people change."

I nodded sympathetically, hoping to find out next his movements on the day of Priyanka's death. Unfortunately, a clerk popped in at that moment with the forms we were waiting for.

I gritted my teeth in disappointment as Mr. Dissanayake

immediately got down to business. After I had filled and signed everything, he rose and escorted us out. "It was nice chatting with you, Mrs. Fernando," he said, unsmiling, as he shut his door.

I rounded on Vino and grabbed her arm in excitement as soon as we exited the building.

"That was suspicious," Vino remarked, beating me to it. "Did you see how his knuckles whitened over his pen when you mentioned Priyanka and blackmail?"

"I did! He nearly snapped that pen in half. No smoke without fire indeed. That's the most extreme reaction we've seen from any of the people we interviewed about Priyanka! I'd say there's a lot of smoke coming from over there. They knew each other from when they were young. And he's in a position of authority, handling money." I lowered my voice. "Could he have stolen from the bank? You know, as in, fraud?"

"I wonder if the police know about their association?" Vino asked. "Should we say something?"

"What? Call the Inspector and say 'Oh, and by the way, I was opening an account at the bank and I just happened to mention Priyanka and the manager almost blew a fuse?'"

Vino mounted her bike and said, "Yes. That's exactly what

we should do. I know the Inspector warned us off, but this is information they need to solve the case. It's not like *we* can look into the bank's accounts or arrest Mr. Dissanayake!"

I felt elated. "I'm sure this is the answer! Of course, we couldn't grill him about an alibi, but… We've solved the case!" I twirled around my bicycle while Vino watched in amusement. "Let's make that call and then get ready to celebrate at Trehan's tonight!"

CHAPTER TEN

THE NIGHT WAS clear and serene as we dove to the new hotel. Trehan met us at the door. His hair was slicked back, he was dressed in a black silk shirt and jeans, and he looked good.

"I have a surprise for you," he said, as he escorted us in. "The new restaurant has been refurbished!" He theatrically flung open the door and announced, "Welcome to Summer Fields!"

The room was dimly lit. Sofas lined each side. Everything was painted a burned orange and yellow. Old fashioned light fixtures adorned the walls. There was one table and three chairs in the centre of the room. Obviously, not all the furniture had arrived. One wall was blank and devoid of any décor. Trehan explained that he had commissioned a large mural to be painted there by a young local artist.

"It's great that you are a patron of local talent," said Vino as we sat down.

The tablecloth was a lovely cream in colour and in the centre was a small vase. Trehan saw me examining it and apologized, saying, "Please excuse the table. I was impatient to christen the restaurant, as it were. Not all the bits and bobs have arrived. I'm getting much finer table centres from Colombo. This is one I had lying around the place."

There were two rolled sheets of cream paper, each tied with a red ribbon, on the table. Vino unfolded one and lifted an eyebrow. "It's handwritten?"

Trehan shrugged. "What can I say? I wanted to have a menu typed out, but my printer cartridge is dry. It'll take days for a new one to arrive from Ratnapura. So, I improvised and wrote it out by hand. I hope you can read my letters!"

"Your writing is beautiful," said Vino as she perused the menu, "for a man!"

We all laughed as he poured some red wine.

"You've pulled out all the stops today!" I remarked, as I took a sip.

"I reckoned we could celebrate!" said Trehan raising his glass. "It's not every day that one evades the clutches of the police!"

"About that," said Vino, setting her glass down. "I want to thank you again for stepping in today even though you had no idea what was going on. You see, when we first realized I was a suspect, we decided to investigate the case on our own so that we had enough information to prove my innocence. And as you saw, that proved to be a really great decision since I was prepared to face their questions at the police station. And we have some exciting news as of this afternoon: we think we know who did it!"

"Really?" he asked, leaning forward. "Why don't you take me through it from the beginning."

So, Vino and I told him how we had been present when the body was discovered; how the police had interviewed her; how we followed up on various leads; and how everyone except Mr. Dissanayake either had no means, no motive, or a cast iron alibi.

"Wait, let me get this straight," said Trehan shaking his head. "You found five suspects? And now you've narrowed it down to just one? You two have been busy the last few days! More efficient than the local police force, I'm sure. A true celebration is in order!"

I blushed as I unrolled my menu. I may as well check out what he had planned for the night. Vino was right, Trehan did have nice handwriting. It also looked oddly familiar. I let my mind wonder as my eyes ran down the page. *Where had I seen writing like this recently?* And then I had it! The letter! The one we had found at the back of Priyanka's book! The signature had been washed out and there was no letterhead, but this handwriting looked awfully similar.

My pulse started to race, and my breathing quickened. I felt the blood drain from my face. I hid my hands on my lap to conceal the shaking. *Could Trehan have written that note? In all our conversations, he never admitted to knowing Priyanka… What was he hiding?* In a daze I realized that my companions had halted their conversation and were looking at me. Vino looked worried.

"Kiy? Are you alright?"

I shook my head, struggled to my feet, and grabbed my handbag. "No, I'm feeling a bit nauseous suddenly. Where's the nearest washroom? Vino, can you come with me, you know, in case I faint or anything?" I knew I was blathering, but I had to speak to her privately.

Trehan led us down a corridor and pointed out the restrooms.

"Sorry to run off like this. We'll be back in a minute," I muttered as I pushed the door in.

I rushed to the nearest wash basin and turned on the tap. Vino watched me in surprise as I splashed my face. I wanted to throw up. My stomach felt genuinely queasy. I also felt cold.

Vino shook me by the shoulders. "Kiy! Are you allergic to the wine?"

That was so ridiculous, I started to laugh. And once I started, I found I could not stop. *I'm getting hysterical!* I grasped the edge of the wash basin. I took a few long, deep breaths and then leaned against a wall. Vino was gaping at me.

"Vino," I said in an urgent whisper. "I think Trehan killed Priyanka!"

"Hold on, *what*?"

"I'm serious. Didn't you recognize the handwriting?" I rummaged in my bag. "Here! Luckily, I'm still carrying this. I thought we could show it to him as part of the celebration..."

I pulled out Priyanka's notebook, which I had thrust into my bag earlier that evening. I flipped it to the end and extracted the letter. "Remember this letter? The handwriting is just like this menu!" I pulled out the menu which I had dropped into my bag as we left the table.

Vino spread both papers out on the washbasin counter. I could see her eye flicking between the two.

"I'm no expert but it looks close. Look at the Ts and the Rs and these Es. I think we need to inform Inspector de Silva. They can get these analysed." She turned to me, a bemused look on her face. "But it's just a letter. We have no proof…"

"Just think about it, Vino!" I interrupted. "They must have *all* studied here together. And when Trehan returned he got in touch with his old school buddies. Only thing was, one of them was a blackmailer! Think of where Priyanka was heading after his meeting with you… walking out of town *in this direction*! We thought someone may have picked him up in a car, but isn't it more likely that he was walking to someplace nearby? Trehan has as much stacked against him as Dissanayake! Come to think of it, I think he has more to lose. We have to tell the police!"

"How? I don't have my phone on me!" Vino's voice was almost a squeak.

"But you called them from outside the bank!"

She slammed her handbag on the washbasin counter. "I plugged it in to charge when we got home. And I cleared out the junk in my bag. Inspector de Silva's visiting card is not in here anymore. We can't call him!"

Every second we spent debating in the bathroom was a second lost. We had to get out of here. *Did Trehan suspect something was up? Was he standing by the door listening to everything we were saying?* I touched Vino on the arm and put a finger to my lips. Then I jerked my head towards the door. She nodded.

We tiptoed to the door and yanked it open. There was no one around. *Where were his staff?* The maid who had brought us our drinks last time, where was she? Surely there must be a waiter and a cook somewhere; we had been invited to dinner after all.

Trying not to think of Chicken Licken and his friends in the fox's lair I pulled Vino down the corridor. We crept past the entrance to the restaurant. Then, I dragged Vino to the large front door and fumbled with the latch to get it open. My fingers seemed to have stopped functioning! After what felt like hours we finally stepped through on to the porch.

We did not get far.

"Are you leaving without saying goodbye?" It was Trehan. He was standing on the front steps. I blinked. He had a gun in his hands!

He waved the weapon at us, steering us away from the front door, back into the house and towards the large armchairs where we had enjoyed a welcome drink what felt like a lifetime ago.

"Take a seat."

Vino and I collapsed into the closest chairs. I wrapped my arms around my stomach. This was not going well.

"You can't keep us here! Someone will come along and find us. What about your staff?" demanded Vino.

"I told them you had left to deal with an emergency and I no longer required their help for the night." He saw the looks on our faces and laughed. "What? Did you expect me to just sit in the restaurant and wait to be caught? Kiyama's reaction was so extreme, I knew the game was up and you suspected something. While you were discussing things in the washroom, I was planning how to get out of this mess." He raised a finger. "And, before you point out the obvious. I moved your car so that the helpers would not see it on their way out. No one knows you are still here."

He sat next to me, so close our thighs were brushing against each other. The gun pressed against my ribs. I closed my eyes, swallowed, and tried not to breathe too hard. "I really liked you, Kiy. You're quirky and intelligent." He lifted his other hand, brushed my hair off my face, and stroked my cheek. "Too clever for your own good."

"Isn't that a bit cliché? I would have got away with it if it were not for you meddling kids etc?"

I wanted to kick Vino. *This was not the time to make lame Scooby Doo jokes!*

I always thought a villain looked, well, villainous when he is found out. Trehan looked his old handsome self. I wanted to pinch myself and see if this were a bad dream. Nice people did not brandish guns. I had been so sure that Trehan was a nice person.

We need to keep him talking until someone arrives.... We need to find a way out!

"Where did you get a gun?" Vino asked.

Of all the questions running through my mind, that was not in the top of the list.

But it worked. He preened and said, "I have to thank you two for the gun! Remember how we first met outside Ariyawansa's building? I made a few inquiries into his business – villagers will talk given the slightest nudge. I contacted him a few days ago and told him I needed an unlicensed weapon for my protection. Living in this mansion with all these valuables can be dangerous. He obliged. You see, I knew that you two were nosing around. I heard you discussing the case at the pool the other day. You really should be more careful whom you trust." He pretended to 'tut tut' in admonishment. "And you should learn to keep your voices down when discussing secrets. But it all worked well for me. And my foresight has served me well, hasn't it?"

"Why did you kill Priyanka?" I whispered. "I want to know. If I am going to die, at least let me die with the satisfaction of having the answer to the riddle."

Vino giggled nervously.

Trehan stood. He began to pace the room, but the gun was always extended in our direction.

"Priyanka." He spat the name out. "You figured out a lot of the story. Dissanayake was not the only one to know Priyanka from his childhood. I was a member of that gang, until I was sent to Colombo. We didn't study in this dingy little town. We were at the most prestigious college in Ratnapura. And I wasn't eight years old when I left, I was in my teens. Oh, we had high larks like all teenagers. But our parents always got us out of trouble. My father, the gem merchant. Priyanka's father was a senior teacher at the school. Dissanayake's was in the local council. And there were the times we didn't get caught." He paused as if recalling all those past misdeeds and smiled. "Those were good times. But, like the little idiots we were, we took photographs. My father bought me a new camera for my thirteenth birthday. You had to develop the roll to see anything those days. Somehow, Priyanka ended up with the worst, most embarrassing pictures. That is what he was holding over our heads. If those got out Dissanayake and I would be the laughingstock of the district. I'm a respected lawyer. I'm trying to set up a business here. Dissa is the bank manager. When I got here a few months ago, and wrote that note wanting to meet up, I had no idea what Priyanka had become. He was already blackmailing Dissa, then. Priyanka showed me the photos. I paid him three times. But it was getting ridiculous! I am tight on funds! My mother doesn't allow me unlimited access to my father's money. She wants to give priority to the gem business."

When he finally stopped his rant, I said, "So, you invited him over and poisoned his drink?"

He smiled thinly. "Priyanka always wanted the better things in life. He resented the fact that we had done so well while he was a mere teacher in a small-town school. I offered him some expensive whisky. The idiot drank it like water! He didn't even taste the insecticide! What a waste of good liquor!"

"You asked him to walk over, didn't you?"

"Yes. I told him I'm paying him for his silence and that includes moving about unnoticed. I didn't want to have to dispose of a bike as well!"

"You thought of everything."

He snorted. "Except that damn notebook! I should have expected an English teacher to keep a diary!"

Suddenly, he stopped pacing and looked at us squarely as we cowered on the sofa.

"And now, I have a second plan to execute. Get up!"

My knees buckled under me as I tried to move. "The police already know about Dissanayake's link to Priyanka. We called them this afternoon from the bank! They'll take him in for questioning. How long do you think he will last? They'll realise you knew Priyanka too. They'll find you eventually!"

I should not have said that. Trehan grabbed my arm and threw me down the corridor leading to the back of the hotel. I crashed into the far wall and landed hard on the floor. My mind went blank as pain shot through me. I heard Vino scream.

"Shut up! Shut the fuck up!"

The next thing I knew, Vino was helping me to my feet. "Don't provoke him!" she whispered. "Keep him talking but don't set him off like that again. Let's try to buy some time…"

"I told you to shut up!" Trehan was right behind us, and I

felt the gun digging into my spine.

We clung to each other as we staggered out the back door. The pool lay in front of us, dark and ominous. *Would he try to drown us? Hold our heads down until we could no longer breathe?* But he directed us to the right. Near the wall was a gaping hole.

"Yes," he said with a cruel laugh. "You can be part of the new foundation of this hotel. Welcome, ladies, to the new changing rooms for the pool. I may have to work late tonight digging it deeper and covering up your existence. The builders are due to finish it off tomorrow. I'll have to make sure they don't look too closely before they pour the concrete. You will make a lovely addition to my new hotel and have a permanent place by my side."

As I stood at the edge of that pit, a terrible sadness enveloped me. *I did not want to die!* Beside me Vino was sobbing quietly.

He held the gun up and took a step back.

I closed my eyes.

"DON'T MOVE! THROW THAT GUN DOWN!"

The shout came from by the wall of the house. Immediately the back lawn lit up. Someone was shining powerful torches straight at us. Blinded, I could not see what was happening. I could hear more voices calling out in the darkness now, and the scuffle of feet.

Suddenly, a shot rang out in the darkness. Vino gave a shriek and toppled into the pit. I felt myself being pulled in after her and prayed that it was not deep.

CHAPTER ELEVEN

A SHARP PAIN stabbed through me. I felt horrible, but I could not feel any bullet wounds. I turned to Vino who was also rising to her feet. "Are you hurt? Did that hit you?"

She shook her head numbly.

We were bathed in mud. The pit was about six feet deep. I tried not to think of newly dug graves. The edge was above eye level, so we could not see what was happening. As Vino and I struggled to find a foothold, a familiar voice called down. "Wait! I'll send someone to help you!"

It was Inspector de Silva.

A policeman leapt into the hole. "Are you injured?"

We both shook our heads, too shocked by the sudden turn of events to speak.

He gave us a smile and a nod. "Don't worry. We'll have you back in the house in no time." Then, he cupped a hand to give us a leg up. Strong arms pulled us out.

Disoriented, I stared around me. The back garden was crawling with police personnel. Some were tying crime scene tape while others were carrying things out of the house. I could see a laptop among the objects being confiscated. In the far corner I recognized the bulky form of Inspector de Silva. He was watching two officers lead Trehan away to the front of the premises. It was satisfying to see that his hands were cuffed, and his head lowered. Hoping that a news reporter was at hand to click multiple embarrassing photographs which would be plastered all over the national tabloids, I allowed the officer to lead me away.

Someone draped a sheet around me and led us back in. The warmth of the cloth and the bright lights emanating from the house lit a comforting glow inside me. I refused to sit in those cursed armchairs in the lobby, so we ended up in the Summer Fields restaurant. The policewoman who brought us mugs of tea informed us that Inspector de Silva will be along soon to speak to us. I cringed inwardly as I thought of everything we had done and hoped he had a sense of humour and a high level of tolerance for amateur investigators.

The dimly lit room and warm sweet tea was making me drowsy. I could feel Vino nodding off beside me. I nudged her awake as Inspector de Silva walked in. He was accompanied by the younger officer who must be his official scribe. "Well, ladies, we have to stop meeting like this!"

Was that a joke? Maybe we were growing on him. "How did you know we were in trouble?" I blurted out.

He smiled. "You have a friend watching out for you, it seems. We received an anonymous tip."

"Thank God you took it seriously!" I said, before I could stop myself. Immediately I wanted to kick myself. The near-death experience must have scrambled my brain.

"Do you have any idea who it was?" Vino inquired. "Trehan sent his staff home when he realized we were on to him. Did one of them, maybe, see him take out the gun? Or guess that we had not left the premises as Trehan claimed and that something was wrong?"

"That's enough idle speculation on your part. We have our suspicions which we will follow up on later." He leaned back.

He looked satisfied that the case was closed, and the murderer was apprehended. Or, it could have been that these chairs were far more comfortable than those found in the interrogation room at the police station.

"Now that that is out of the way," he said, "perhaps you can fill me in as to how you ended up on the edge of that pit?"

Vino and I took it in turns to explain. We omitted nothing. I handed him the menu, the letter and Priyanka's notebook. We recounted everything Trehan had admitted to us while pacing the lobby. Between the two of us we were able to recall his words almost verbatim.

Inspector de Silva nodded while his colleague wrote reams of notes. "Well," he said when we were finally done. "I have got to hand it to you. You were thorough. I only wish you had shared all this when you called me this afternoon. We could have avoided all this chaos."

"But we thought Mr. Dissanayake was the killer, we did inform you of that. And we didn't know the significance of the letter at that point," I noted.

"Yes, there is that." He regarded us severely. "I could charge you with obstruction of justice, you know. That notebook you found. It should have been handed in immediately. You not only intercepted it you also encouraged that girl to lie for you!"

I decided to eat humble pie and nodded. "Yes, Inspector. I'm sorry. It won't happen again…"

"I should hope not!" His brow cleared and he smiled. "You came very close to losing your lives tonight. Don't forget that."

I gulped. That was one experience I was unlikely to ever forget.

As he rose to leave, he said, "There's an ambulance waiting to take you to the local hospital." He lifted an index finger as we started to object. "You may feel fine, but that was a dramatic tumble. You can thank whatever deity you pray to that the pit was empty of the workmen's tools and you have no spinal injuries. Also, you haven't looked at yourselves in a mirror yet."

Vino and I exchanged startled glances. *Did we look that bad?*

"Once the doctors discharge you a police car will drive you back to Komarika Lodge. It's inadvisable for you to drive in your condition. We've had enough misadventures for one night. I'll have an officer bring your car over."

"Thank you so much, Inspector," we chorused.

"Remember my advice: don't pull any more stunts like this. Just enjoy your vacation."

With that parting shot he turned and walked out.

My body was black and blue the next day. That is one disadvantage of having fair skin – your minor injuries are painted for the whole world to see. I found it difficult to move. Nevertheless, I was thankful we had escaped with a few bruises and no broken bones. Or worse. The doctor who had checked our health last night said I was in bad shape compared to Vino, but I had no broken ribs and no internal injuries. He gave me some pain killers and recommended bed rest for a few days.

However, I am not one to laze around, so I gingerly swung my legs out of bed. My agonized cries brought Manike rushing into my room.

"Are you alright, Miss?" she gasped, holding me up by my arm.

"Yes, yes, as fine as can be expected," I muttered. "Here, help me move, will you?"

I shuffled like an octogenarian out of my room and into the hall. Vino was already seated at the dining table. She and Manike helped me take a seat.

"Oww…" I gasped, as I lowered myself into the chair. "Is there a walker or wheelchair lying around by any chance?" *How am I going to eat anything?* I winced as I lifted the cutlery to my mouth. "You seem to be moving just fine," I commented after I watched Vino for a few minutes.

"You took the brunt of the beating, remember? I kept my mouth shut."

"Yes, yes. Me and my big mouth," I smiled at her. "At least we filled in all the missing details and solved the crime!"

"And caught a criminal!"

"Well, technically, he caught us, and then the police caught him, but who cares." I swallowed my breakfast with difficulty. "That doctor said I had no broken ribs, right? Or was I hallucinating?"

Vino laughed, and then clutched her back. "Don't make me laugh!"

We were both clutching our sides when Kumar walked in. He was juggling two bouquets of flowers, and a box of chocolates.

"Kumar!" we exclaimed as we accepted the gifts, "how nice of you to drop by! How did you know we were in need of some good cheer?"

"Vino called first thing in the morning and said she won't be coming in to work because of a minor emergency." He put both hands on his hips. "A minor emergency? You look like you've been run over by a train!" He held up a hand. "It's okay. I should have known you would catch the guy even at the risk of your own lives. By the way, your exploits are all over town. People will be talking of this murder and the aftermath for the next few decades!"

"Hey, we're famous!" Vino said as she tucked into the sweets.

"More like infamous," I commented as I joined her. "Mmm… These are heavenly, Kumar. Which angel inspired you to bring us convalescents chocolates?"

He grinned. "My wife. She says there's nothing a box of chocolates can't fix. And speaking of infamous, you may not be able to continue teaching at the school…"

"Oh, my gosh, I forgot to call in and excuse myself today!" I gasped, my hands flying to my face.

"That's what I'm trying to tell you. Mrs. Palpola called and said they are getting a replacement English teacher next week and they can manage for the next few days. She asked you to come and collect your cheque at the end of the month for the days you worked."

"What?" I said, in disbelief. "They want me to leave after teaching for just two days? That timing is fortuitous. Something tells me they were glad to see me go. Perhaps, they don't approve of their teachers catching criminals!"

"Of course not!" joked Vino. "Teachers are pillars of respectability. First Priyanka gets himself bumped off. Then, you almost get yourself buried. I mean, come on, they are probably praying for normalcy right about now."

"Or else," I said, "the post is cursed!"

"Don't-make-me-laugh!" gasped Vino, again, as Kumar let out a guffaw.

Soon, he stood up to take our leave. "I need to get back to the office and let everyone know you are okay," he said. "And don't worry, we can manage without you. Don't ride that bike for at least a week!"

We followed his advice and took it easy for the next few days. My bruises eventually disappeared, and my good mood reasserted itself. Before long I was raring to leave the confines of the house.

"Let's drive in to Eheliya again on Saturday," I proposed. "We're running short of muesli again."

Eheliya town was much larger than Parkaduwa, but nothing compared to Colombo. I realized I was feeling homesick. I missed the large shopping malls, the coffee shops, large public parks, and fancy restaurants. I was not one to frequent night clubs, but I had enjoyed meeting friends for a meal, or a movie. Perhaps, we could go down to Colombo for the day.

We made the most of what was available. We spent a few lazy hours browsing through the clothes shops and having a turbid cup of coffee at a small café. Then we visited the supermarket and selected all the goodies that are unavailable back home.

Home. Funny that I was starting to think of Komarika Lodge as home.

Finally, we took a break at the children's park before driving back. Leaving our purchases in the car, we strolled along the tree lined pathways and rested on a cement bench by a small pond. Families picnicked on the grass enjoying the weekend.

"I wonder what will happen to Trehan's hotel now," I mused aloud, as I watched two boys play football nearby.

"His mother will either complete the renovations, or sell the place, is my guess," answered Vino.

"Such a pity. It was shaping up to be a really nice place. I hope whoever buys it finishes the work. Also, I'm sure the town and surrounding villages could do with the additional jobs it would provide."

"You've given this some thought, haven't you?"

"Yes. But don't worry. I don't have nearly enough money to buy it myself!"

"Let's wait and see. Perhaps you could join the staff in some capacity if you are keen. Maybe as an events manager? Or a trainer for all the new staff they have to hire from the village?"

I liked the sound of that. After teaching poetry and drama for fifteen years, a change of occupation and a change of pace would be welcome.

We lapsed into a companionable silence. I recalled my vision of visitors cycling along the narrow lanes, and participating in cookery classes, and smiled.

"I suppose Trehan will make bail and leave the country," I ventured after a while.

Vino shrugged. "That's the way these things work. Even when the guy is caught, it takes so many years for the case to go through the court system. Those who can make bail don't stick around. He is a lawyer, after all. He'll know how to bend the rules."

"If he is let out, even for a short time, I sincerely hope he doesn't come back to plague us," I said with a shiver.

"I'm sure Inspector de Silva will see to it that he doesn't bother us."

"He's not that bad, is he?" I asked, gazing at some children playing with a dog.

"Who? The Inspector? No, he's not that bad after all."

A surprise awaited us at our return. Manike had propped up an envelope on the dining table. It had no stamp and no address.

"Manike, where did this come from?" Vino called into the kitchen.

"I don't know, Miss. I was cooking all morning. Then, I went out to talk to Somasiri and saw this on one of the chairs in the veranda. Someone must have kept it there."

We sat at the table and opened it. A card dropped out. It was a plain white board. On it was typed:

Two favours delivered.

I will call in my debts.

"Is it signed?" I asked flipping it over. There was a small capital letter A on one side.

"Ariyawansa!" Vino gasped her face white. "He's the only one to whom we owe a favour!"

"He mentions two favours, though," I pointed out. Then the puzzle fell into place. "Wait, could *he* have phoned in that tip to the police? That evening we were at Trehan's?"

"Yes!"

"Trehan said he purchased the gun from Ariyawansa. Maybe they were keeping an eye on him. There's only room for one master criminal in a place like this, after all."

Vino shuddered. "I don't like this. He knows where we live, and he has obviously kept an eye on our movements. And now he wants to call in his debts at a future date… Should we inform the police?"

I considered it. "No, there's nothing to go on right now. If he asks us to do something illegal, then we'll call the cops." I laughed. "At this rate, we'll have Inspector de Silva on speed dial!"

Vino did not answer, so I turned and looked at her, my eyebrows raised in a silent question.

"You said 'us'. Thank you for standing by me in this, Kiy,"

she finally said, giving me a hug.

"Of course it's 'us'!" I retorted. "We got into this together and we have to see it through!"

Just then, my phone pinged. I looked at the screen, and nearly dropped the device.

Vino noticed my reaction and grew pale. "Is it Trehan? Is he sending you threatening messages?"

"I wish!" I shook my head. "It's Andy! I walked out weeks ago. There wasn't a hum from him. No call, no email. Nothing. And he drops me a message now?"

"Check what he wants."

I opened the text:

Missing you.

Give me a call.

I buried my head in my hands. *Just as I had settled down to a new life, this had to happen! First Ariyawansa, and now Andy. Why?*

Vino placed a hand on my shoulder. "Just leave it for now. Give it some thought before you answer 'yes' or 'no'. In the meantime, how about a movie?"

ABOUT THE AUTHOR

Nadishka Aloysius is a teacher, actor, and author. Being a teacher of Drama and English Language with twenty years' experience, and a mother of two sons who love story time, she finds inspiration in the little everyday details of life. Nadishka loves reading crime fiction and fantasy and this is reflected in her writing for Tween, YA, and adult audiences. She conducts creative writing workshops and school visits to share her love of literature. As an actor she prefers to play the antagonist since it allows her to explore the darker sides of human nature. The picture book *Roo The Little Red Tuk Tuk* was a Finalist at the Wishing Shelf Book Award. Her debut novel for children *Ronan's Dinosaur* was shortlisted for the State Literary Awards in 2019, while her first YA novella *Raavana's Daughter* was longlisted for the prestigious Gratiaen Award in 2020. *That Easter Sunday* was awarded Best Children's Literature Category II at the State Literary Awards 2021.

Other books by this author:
For Pre-Schoolers

Toran and the Alphabet Fairy
Roo, the Little Red Tuk Tuk
Eyesha and the Great Elephant Gathering
The Little Lost Fishing Cat
Dressing Up with Archchi
Working Out with Mama (Coming Soon)
Ayash Grows a Family Tree (Coming Soon)

For Middle Grade readers
Ronan's Dinosaur
That Easter Sunday
Travel Journal for Kids

For Teenagers

Raavana's Daughter
Gratitude Prayer Journal

For Adults

The Body in the Paddy Field
Murder at the Wedding
Death at the Fete
Corpses in Colombo

Find Nadishka Aloysius Books on    

ACKNOWLEDGEMENTS

This book would not be possible without the contribution of many people.

My heartfelt thanks go out to my family for their support, especially to my husband Rajeev for his feedback on the manuscript.

I would also like to thank Devika Brendon for taking the time to edit the manuscript. And my special thanks go out to Gimara Goonawardene and Sachini Seneviratne for their invaluable advice.

READ ON FOR A TASTE OF GRATIAEN AWARD NOMINATED

RAAVANA'S DAUGHTER...

Mermaids, Demons, Gods...It is 8000 years B.C. Sita Devi, the wife of Lord Rama, the Prince of Ayodhya, has been abducted by the Demon King Raavana. Hanuman, the Ape hero, is tasked with building a bridge to facilitate the invasion of Lanka. The Ape army gathers on the Southern coast of India. The expedition is however brought to a halt by the workings of the Mer-People who inhabit the Indian Ocean.

Follow Hanuman as he struggles to overcome their enchantments and complete his task. However, who is the mysterious Mer-Queen who lures him into her undersea lair? What part has she to play in this epic war? Is all fair in love and war?

CHAPTER SIX

Hanuman was appalled to see Mermaids active in the ocean around the island. There was no record of them inhabiting the waters of South India, and no seamen had reported a sighting - which, of course, did not mean they did not exist. Quickly, Hanuman formulated a plan. He was on his own. He needed to gather intelligence about the creatures in order to deal with the problem. Then he would have to uncover some magic or a talisman that would dispel the Mermaids. To do that, he would have to follow them into the water.

Hanuman had many powers. As a child he had acquired many boons from gods. Unfortunately, since he had used his new-found powers for mischief a great sage had cursed him, erasing all remembrance of them. When he was commanded to assist Lord Rama the curse was lifted. One power had already served him well in this war - the ability to fly. Another, yet unused, was the ability to survive underwater for a length of time. It was on this that he pinned his hopes as he dove into the water.

He swam with powerful strokes towards the shimmering light which improved visibility under water and turned the seabed into a floodlit garden. The floor was carpeted in multi-coloured corals. Fish of all sizes darted in and out, seemingly undisturbed by the activity around them. Hanuman was careful to stay away from the razor-sharp edges of the coral reef as he made his way towards the bridge.

The bridge was a wonder to behold, floating above him like one of the King's roads that meandered through the countryside. It was broad enough for four horse drawn carts travelling abreast. He took a circuitous route towards the mermaids, who were too preoccupied with the destruction to notice his arrival. Hiding behind a large rocky outcrop, Hanuman observed more closely these fantastic creatures of the deep.

They were playful and terrible to watch. They were childlike as if joyfully breaking down a toy they had built themselves. They tossed the boulders between them in a game of catch. Hanuman noticed subtle differences in their size and shape, and realised that both male and female of the species were present. Some of the larger Mer-People used their strong tails to swat aside rocks and it soon became clear they were competing to see who could throw one the farthest.

Hanuman scanned the assembled crowd trying to decipher a command structure. Who was in charge of the mayhem? He noticed a group floating by the side of the bridge. The Mer-People formed a circle around a Mermaid who was more magnificent than the others. Her strong features were not as severe and her form was lithe. She was bedecked in pearls polished until they reflected the light. Her tail shimmered as if she wore cloth of gold interwoven with precious jewels. A crown of coral was on her lustrous hair, which streamed around her like a cloak. In her hand she grasped a trident.

He had found the Mer-Queen.

www.ingramcontent.com/pod-product-compliance
Lightning Source LLC
LaVergne TN
LVHW020744200726
843506LV00009B/869